"If it's wearing pants, or may not be a monkey."

Monkeys Wearing Pants

Funny rants, riffs and meaningless musings by a guy you don't know

2nd Edition

By Jon Waldrep

Copyright © 2019 Jon Waldrep

All rights reserved.

No part of this publication may be reproduced, stored in a retrieval system, or transmitted, in any form or by any means without permission of the author.

Table of Contents

Intro iv

A Tinkle of Random Stuff 1

A Weighty Notion 7

Facebook, Computers and Technology, Oh My 21

Randomness 31

Famous Last Words 39

Getting Older 43

Travel 53

More Random Randomness 71

Jobs & Working 85

We Are Family 95

This Is the End. The Final Random-O-Rama-Dama 105

Severodvinsk – a mostly true travel story 123

Barbara Ham from Canada 153

The Coldest Shower in Morocco 197

Greetings!

First of all, thank you for taking the time to check out my eBook (note to self: I have just royally screwed myself over if this ever gets published as a printed book). I would like to say that I slaved over a hot computer for years to write this, but that wouldn't be true. Rather, this is more like a casserole you put together at the last minute when you are trying to get rid of things in the fridge before they start looking like a sixth-grade science experiment gone terribly awry. I don't know if that makes sense, but now I'm worried that I am just making you hungry rather than talking about the literary feast you are about to indulge in. OK, maybe not a feast. Think pigs-in-a-blanket and a Home Depot bucket filled with cheap Sangria.

I have cobbled together things that I have written for blogs, things I have posted on Facebook, restroom wall scrawlings and some nuggets from letters I received while in prison. Just kidding about that last part. I never got a single letter in prison. OK, I confess, I have never actually even been close to being in prison except for that time I tried to break into the women's prison in Chowchilla, California for a Sadie Hawkins dance that I was not actually invited to attend. Yes, a major social faux pas and apparently a felony if caught.

But I digress.

I hope you enjoy this. If I can make you chuckle a few times, I'll be happy. If I can get you to spit up coffee mid-sip because you read something you found to be really funny, I will do a victory dance around my sofa (like three times, let's not go crazy here). In any case hopefully there is something you find amusing because, frankly, that is the point. If you enjoy reading it half as much as I enjoyed writing it, then we have created a new math problem that will freeze some kid's brain.

Thanks again,

Jon Waldrep jmwaldrep@gmail.com

Update

But wait! There's more! This is the new and updated version of Monkeys Wearing Pants. It is now bigger, better and fortified with iron! I've added a lot more good stuff, taken out some not-so-good stuff and included an original short story and a non-fiction travel piece. I hope you like it. If you do, please feel free to write a glowing review, clearly mentioning how I have made your life worth living again. If you don't like it then you are dead to me. Just kidding. No, I'm really not. Anyway, happy reading. See you in the funny papers. — Jon

A Tinkle of Random Stuff

News flash! There is a lot of random stuff in here. I tried to make categories for everything, but after making the category, 'famous sayings related to razor burn and a major religion' I realized I had gone too far. I had pushed the envelope, literally, all the way to the 'pushing the envelope' category. I will invite you, if you are so inclined, to put every random passage into an imaginary category of your own invention. This is particularly fun if you sublet a basement in your mom and dad's home and have no real friends.

If cars were like printers, you could buy a new Chevy for $1,000, but gas would be $50 a gallon.

I woke up this morning having a major existential crisis. I questioned if my life had meaning, purpose or value. Then I ate an everything bagel and was fine.

If I accidentally called you today, I'm sorry. I'd like to say I "butt dialed" you, but my phone was in my front pocket. Awkward.

Man, if I had a quarter for every time I said, "Man, if I had a quarter for every time…" (rinse and repeat).

I have been writing to a lot of women in prison. I should have a date in five to ten years. Three with good behavior.

I would travel to a parallel universe, but I wouldn't want to park there.

Listen, I do think your girlfriend is hot. But it's a dry heat.

Do you like the sound of heavy metal? Then come over and listen as I apply the brakes on my car.

The other day I bought a couple of lottery scratchers. I didn't win, but I gave myself a really nice participation trophy.

The other day I was baking and I began to speak weirdly. I think I just got a yeast inflection.

I just used a gender-neutral restroom. It was really hard to leave the toilet seat at a 45-degree angle.

Only 54 shopping days left until Dewey Decimal System Day!

I ran into Elsa the other day. I hate to say it, but she's really let herself go.

I believe in the time-honored tradition of letting the dirty dishes soak overnight. Or for a day or two. Or until I have to bury them out back. Whatever. Don't judge.

I started to invent programmable underwear with an auto-cool feature and high-tech ventilation system. Then I decided it was easier to just go naked.

Getting ready to head into a 2-hour sexual harassment training at work. I don't really think I need it. I can only hope that it's given by a super-hot chick.

If I say I'm going to do something, I do it. I don't need your constant, nagging reminders every 12-18 months.

My efforts to learn a third language, after English and Spanish, have not gone well. Having said that, I'm pretty sure I could find the library in several other countries.

I only go to one dentist, so I have no idea what the other four are recommending.

A TINKLE OF RANDOM STUFF

The other morning a co-worker told me it was National Wine Day, so I complained non-stop.

I want to get a pet dog and name it Peeve.

I adopted a highway, but it left to find its biological interstate.

I want to turn over a new leaf. I'm thinking fig...

It sounds crazy, but I can make it rain whenever I want. All I have to do is wash my car.

Becoming a father really changed my life. Imagine never having to bend over to pick something up again. Kids really are little miracles. Little, low-to-the-ground, super flexible miracles.

I killed two birds, but I had to use two stones to do it. Proverb merit badge out the window...

MacGyver could make any problem go away with a paperclip and a roll of duct tape. I can do the same thing with three or four beers.

I was in a medically induced coma recently. No. Wait. I just watched an Adam Sandler movie on Netflix. Never mind.

Why does there have to be any way to skin a cat?

It's kind of sad that my kids will never know the satisfaction of slamming down the phone at the end of an angry phone conversation.

I finally exercised my demons. They're in pretty good shape now and entered in a zombie half-marathon.

In the great tradition of Boxing Day, I just decked the guy in the next cubicle with a right cross.

Some people like to catch fish when they're spawning. I like to catch fish when they're spamming. I use click bait.

Father-daughter dance with my daughters tonight. Or, as I like to call it, awesome opportunity to embarrass my kids in front of their friends. Funky Chicken, anyone?

I'm slightly color blind, so sometimes I have a hard time distinguishing brown from black. Aside from the occasional poor sock choice, it doesn't really have any major, real world consequences. The upside is that no matter how the toast comes out, I'm probably going to eat it.

I finally broke down and bought a new shower caddy. It works great but keeps insisting I play the loofah when I would rather lay-up with the wash cloth.

I almost dislocated my shoulder trying to open a jar of pickles. Either I'm getting weaker, or the members of the local pickle packing union have really upped their game.

I just bought a new trash can. Huh. I guess I do have disposable income after all.

The only time I want somebody's two-cents worth is when I buy something for a little less than a dollar.

There's something about erasing my browsing data since the beginning of time that makes me feel just a little all-powerful and omnipotent.

At the end of each day, everyone at work makes a beeline to the restroom before they have to hit the road to go home. I call it 5 o'clock flush hour.

A TINKLE OF RANDOM STUFF

I hate to be overtly political, but can both parties please come together and work on the common cause of a standardized size for a paper towel sheet?

Sometimes I think it's time to get back out there and start dating again. Then I remember that relationships are really just two people constantly asking each other what they want to eat, until one of them dies.

After significant time together, my toilet paper plies have decided to separate.

A Weighty Notion

I write a lot about weight, mostly because I have an abundance of it to write about. While I don't need to buy airplane seats two at a time (or even use the dreaded seat belt extender), the little tray on the plane can leave an indentation in my stomach that lasts for days. In any case, I understand the yo-yo weight gain and loss that comes with trying a never-ending variety of diets.

They say that periodic fasting is good for you so I'm going to try it. Probably between meals.

Second day of my fast. I looked down and for a second and I thought I could see a toe! But it was just a piece of pretzel I dropped last week.

17 hours into my fast. I feel hungry, and like I should be giving a urine sample somewhere.

More than 24 hours into my fast. Going pretty well. My sofa looks like a giant cheesecake.

I'm following the lead of my friend and will be fasting on Monday and Tuesday. On Wednesday I'll be at the local buffet from 11:00 AM until 4:00.

I kind of wish my body was more portrait mode, and less landscape.

I want to lose weight, but I want to do it my way, the right way, like if being in a prolonged coma or losing a limb at lumberjack fantasy camp.

Some people have an hour-glass figure. I'm more of a traditional sun dial.

The bad thing about living in England is if you wake up one morning and proclaim that you, "feel like a million pounds!" - no one knows if you just feel really great, or if you're going to have to wear your fat pants.

When I'm stressed, I overeat. When I overeat, I get fat. When I'm fat, I get stressed. I feel like a rock that has, "Turn me over" painted on both sides.

I'm trying to lose some weight, but you know what they say, the last 87 pounds are the hardest.

I'm getting ready to start a new diet. I can only eat foods with hard consonants. I don't think it will be that difficult, although I may need to take a remedial English class first.

You know you have to lose weight when your fat pants send you a cease and desist order.

Telling someone that I have lost 5 pounds is kind of like saying, "Hey, did you notice that Mt. Everest is 7 feet shorter!"

I tried to measure my thigh gap. That's one ruler I'm never getting back.

When your "fat"' clothes start getting snug, you know you have a problem. Getting dressed this morning was like trying to squeeze an eggplant into a condom.

Good news! I have already made my lunches for the next three days. Bad news? I'm still pathologically incapable of accurately measuring pasta.

A WEIGHTY NOTION

I am now a proud member of Overeaters Anonymous. Hmmm, I guess now that I posted this publicly, I'm just an overeater.

I'm glad I don't have to hunt for my own food. I don't even know where pizzas live.

My head and face look like the aftermath of an accident at the Silly Putty factory.

They say that as little as 2 ounces of chocolate a day can offer great health benefits. That means I'm good to go until 2033!

We had a meeting at work where I was given some food for thought. It went right to my bottom line.

I'm the opposite of fun sized.

So today I made a serious, new dieting plan. It's a lot easier to commit to a major diet after eating a super carnitas burrito with everything.

I have got to lose some weight. I either need the world's greatest diet, or the world's strictest girlfriend.

I have started juicing to lose weight. It's going OK, but cleaning those donut crumbs out of the juicer is a pain.

Today was National Brownie Day or, as I like to say, forget the doctor, dentist, dietitian and scale day.

When I come out as fat I think a lot of people are going to be caught by surprise.

Signs that you need to lose weight:

1. You need an oxygen tank nearby after you put on your socks.

2. You're willing to risk dislocating your shoulder for that French fry that fell under your seat in your car.
3. Little kids point at you and say, "Look, Mommy! Bounce house!"
4. Your bathroom scale flashes obscenities when you climb on it.
5. You are looking at the "People of Wal-Mart" website and see a butt crack that looks very, very familiar.
6. They give you four sets of plastic utensils with a takeout order that's only for you.
7. You finish off that large pizza while sitting on the toilet.
8. The only way you can keep your shirt tucked into the front is to super glue the bottom to your pubic hair.
9. You see a $20 bill on the ground and debate whether it's worth bending over to pick it up.
10. They make you sign a waiver at the all-you-can-eat buffet.

Most people don't like it when they start to get a gut. But then it grows on them.

I have got to lose some weight. I mean, I could probably handle a couple more pounds, but I just don't want to get any jollier.

I just lost like 8 pounds. I have no idea where I put that suitcase.

I'm either going to join a gym or take part in a pie eating contest. The pros and cons are all over the place on this one.

I tried the massage chair at the gym today. It was so good, I'm tempted to change my Facebook status to, "In a relationship."

A WEIGHTY NOTION

Twinkies are back, thank God. There just aren't enough high calorie snacks made from cellulose gum, Sodium stearate and calcium sulfate. And where else can you get a creamy filling made of shortening and Polysorbate 60? Yummers!!

A friend has convinced me to try this lemon juice detox regimen. It calls for drinking a mixture of water, lemon juice, cayenne pepper and maple syrup. You drink it for ten days... or until your ass falls off. I'm going to try it, but I think I am going to substitute beer for the water, lemon drops for the lemon juice, spicy chicken wings for the cayenne pepper and maple bars for the syrup. Wish me luck!

I now officially weigh enough to where strangers think sympathetically, "Oh, good for him!" when they see me walking around on my breaks.

Pick-up lines for fat guys:

1. In case you were wondering, yes, I am jolly as Hell.
2. If you want, we can go do laundry together. I have a whole roll of quarters where my belly button used to be.
3. No promises, but after rolling around with me, most women say their cellulite flattens out nicely.
4. Just close your eyes and pretend you're making out with two moderately stocky guys.
5. Think! Dinner and a movie with a fat guy has to be somewhere on your bucket list!
6. I want to get hot and sweaty. I would just rather get that way with another person in the same room.

Is it large, all-meat pizza for a cold and 24-hour-buffet for a fever, or the other way around?

Sure, I read food labels and I give them the same thought and consideration that I would a zit in the middle of my back. I know it's there, but it's not going anywhere and I really can't do anything about it.

This month, I've decided that I'm not going to eat meat, fast food, candy, overdo it on carbs or drink alcohol. I'm also going to the gym every day at lunch. I know that sounds like overkill, so to balance it out, I'll be starting a crack cocaine habit.

Went to the gym today. I'm not going to say exactly how many calories I burned, but if I keep going like this in about three months I'll be able to eat a Tic Tac -- guilt free!

Going to the gym is not for everyone. I say if you really hate the gym, don't go. Not going is better than driving in circles around the parking lot until the parking space right next to the entrance opens up.

If you spend an hour watching TV from a treadmill going so slowly it makes the revolving restaurant at the top of the Seattle Space Needle seem like a demonic roller coaster ride, then you really shouldn't bother going to the gym at all.

Holy crapola, when did I gain all of this weight? One day you look in the mirror and see a distressing version of the Michelin Tire Man looking back at you. Where once you might have been lean and mean, you now find that your gut hangs over your belt like a deployed airbag and your ass has become an overfilled waterbed mattress that rolls in and out like the tide.

Five things that are going to happen if I don't start losing weight:

A WEIGHTY NOTION

1. People are going to start calling me saying, "Dude! I just saw you on Google Earth!"
2. The lights will mysteriously go out, and the front door will lock when I pull into the all-you-can-eat Chinese buffet.
3. I will get offers to be the "before" picture for the latest diet pill.
4. The only pants I'll be able to wear are my faux jean sweatpants.
5. The bungee jumping company will have me sign a release and sell me life insurance before I jump.

Will the gremlin that is sneaking into my house and systematically taking in the waists on all of my pants please cease and desist?

Fat guy autopilot: when you go to the store for kale but come home with tater-tots and a pound cake.

I love those 100-calorie packs of cookies, crackers and sweets. I think they are a great way to satisfy your sweet tooth without overdoing it. And the cool thing is that you can keep track of the calories just by doing some pretty simple math. Every day, I eat exactly 100 of those bags because I know that's only... hang on...carry the 1....100 of those bags is only...hmmm... wait a minute! OH CRAP!

There is now always a tub of Red Vines at work. It's hard not to eat them, but I'm going to kick the Red Vine habit; I'll probably start with a patch.

We started a *Biggest Loser*-type competition at work today and had our official first weight in. Ironically, today I chose to wear my lead-lined briefs, 1978 platform shoes and a soaking wet alpaca sweater. I'm not saying that I'm trying to give myself an unfair advantage, but I WILL WIN!

I'm thinking of starting this all-garlic diet. Nothing but raw garlic, cooked garlic, and food cooked with an abundance of garlic. I don't really think I'll lose weight, but I'm pretty sure I'll look slimmer from a distance.

My doctor says I need to lose 50 pounds, so yesterday I started using the Wii Fit again. Instead of the cheerful, animatronic greeting I remembered, I was greeted with, "What the hell! Do you think you can just waltz back here after all this time and start over? Do you? Well, let me tell you something, buddy boy, it doesn't work that way! Where have you been? You heard me! Where the hell have you been? Well? I'm waiting!" I guess it's been a while.

When it's cool to lie about your weight: your driver's license.

When it's not such a good idea to lie about your weight: pre zip-line information form.

A few more signs that you may need to lose weight:

1. Baby ducks instinctively line up and follow you when you walk by a pond.
2. You made the mistake of getting a booth instead of a table at your favorite restaurant, and they needed the jaws-of-life to extract you.
3. Your ass is big enough to affect weather patterns and may be contributing to global warming.
4. Great Britain and Argentina are both considering claiming your land mass as sovereign territory.
5. You have ever eaten anything resembling a 5th grade science experiment you found hidden away in the back of your fridge.

A WEIGHTY NOTION

6. You've pretended to be on your cell phone while at a Chinese takeout to "ask your friend" what they wanted when you were really just getting a second order for you.
7. You've had two theme park attendants pushing down on your roller coaster safety bar with all their strength, so it will lock in place.
8. You have more than four pizza delivery places on speed dial.
9. A flight attendant has moved you to another seat to "balance the load."
10. You have had to lie on the floor and use a pair of pliers to zip up your jeans.

I have got to lose some weight. I know that as a man I can't get pregnant, but my BMI suggests that I am eating for two.

You know you need to lose weight if you have to consult the Kama Sutra just to figure out how you're going to put your socks on.

The worst part of selling one of your old pieces of exercise equipment is when the prospective buyer looks at it, then looks at you and asks, "And you're sure this thing works, right?"

I think I need to enter Rice Crispy Treat rehab. Yes, the first step is admitting you have a problem.

I don't think that sodium is that bad for you. Sodium means salt. Salt comes from the sea. Man evolved from the sea. We started out as little sea monkeys and then evolved into walking fish, standing fish, giddy, little newts, lizards, cab drivers, monkeys, monkeys who started parting their hair on the right and, finally, people. Salt is good. The Bible even talks about salt and gives it two holy thumbs up. So, when you are reading that label, remember that sodium is literally the salt of the earth and good for you. Keep beer handy.

Why do stores stock packaged, men's dress shirts smallest on the top and then all the way down to the really big sizes? The little guys can't reach that high and the fat guys don't want to bend over.

A few weeks ago, I was working in the backyard on a hot, sunny day and got fried. Sadly, my weight remained unchanged after cooking.

I usually try and walk during my lunch break, but today it was pouring rain so to compensate I did an extra lap around the all-you-can-eat Indian buffet table.

Once again, I find myself mired in the whole teaspoon/tablespoon conundrum. Honest to God, which is which? I have a drawer full of different sized spoons but the only one I can identify with certainty is my over-sized cereal-bowl spoon. I know this because it is proportionate to the salad bowl I use for my Frosted Mini Wheats. As for the rest of those spoons and my general confusion, I blame the metric system or maybe the British, for not knowing which spoon to use to make the medicine go down.

I did an oil painting of an overweight friend. Now I'm being accused of fat-framing.

I wolfed down two slices of all meat pizza, a couple of hot peppers and a diet soda. I'm pretty sure for the next couple of hours, my carbon footprint was a lot bigger than size 11 wide.

It's not the midnight snacking that gets me, it's honoring all of the time zones. Hey, it's twelve o'clock somewhere.

A WEIGHTY NOTION

Came upon a pair of 32-inch pants in my closet. I looked at the pants. The pants looked at me. Then we laughed and laughed. Those were good times.

My Body Mass Index is totally screwed up. I'm supposed to be 6' 6" tall? Yeah, right.

I have a chart that shows you how many calories you burn doing various activities like swimming, jogging, playing tennis, etc. Nowhere on there does it even mention walking from the living room to the bedroom looking for a ROKU remote.

I'm in terrible shape; every time I tie my shoes I want to shout out, "Feel the burn!"

In my life movie where I am trying to lose weight, pizza is the villain who ties me to the tracks and laughs in my face.

Gluttony is a sin, but as it turns out my diet of nothing but deviled eggs isn't going to save me.

I tied a piece of string cheese around my finger to remind me to eat less dairy.

I grabbed something this morning that I wasn't sure I should wear, but I did because the sum of the pants was greater than the hole.

I want to lose just enough weight to not be jolly.

I'm trying to cut back, so from now on I'm only going to go with about half a kit and caboodle, maybe just seven of the nine yards, and only a healthy dollop of the whole shebang. I'm still going to eat the whole enchilada though.

I like this high fiber, zero sugar cereal I bought, but I'm not sure why they had to make look like rat droppings. Although when you think about it, I guess you don't see a lot of out-of-shape rats not getting enough fiber in their diets.

An optimist looks in a refrigerator and sees it as half full. A pessimist looks but says it is half empty. I look and say, "What is this stuff turning green in the Tupperware container behind the condiments?"

I made the mistake of eating a large bowl of cereal last night before bed. I snapped and crackled most of the night and this morning I finally popped.

I saw a homeless guy peddling his bike downtown and had mixed emotions. On one hand, I thought about how sad it was that this guy didn't have a place to call home. On the other hand, I was jealous of the fact that the guy had about 2% body fat.

It's been a lot of hard work. A lot of sacrifice. A great deal of going above and beyond, but I've finally gotten to the place where I am ready to take my "before" picture.

I was going to pick-up Chinese food for dinner tonight but then decided against it. You know what they say though, and sure enough a half-hour later I decided against it again.

I think it's great that there are so many new, high-tech, fitness trackers. Now you can track, with incredible accuracy and pinpoint precision, all those workouts you never do.

I was going to count calories today, but then I had some Canadian bacon and the exchange rate screwed me up.

Going forward, I'm only going to eat range free cookies. Roam free my oatmeal raisin friends! Roam free!

A WEIGHTY NOTION

I hate brushing my teeth at night because that signifies that you can't have any more food and I'm just never ready for that kind of commitment.

Starting tomorrow I'm going to lay off the carbs. Yes, I will be handing a bagel a pink slip.

I'm going to eat a whole person, so if anyone gives me a hard time about eating too much I can say, "Hey! I'm eating for two here!"

Sadly, I've come to the conclusion that carbs really don't love me at all. They just use me to get to my ass.

Man, I am just one, good case of food poisoning away from making my weight goal this month!

Why aren't there any chubby stick people?

Hi everyone. Here's a quick cooking tip for you. When preparing kale make sure you use plenty of oil. That makes it a lot easier to scrape it into the trash later.

If I was super rich I would hire a personal trainer, and then I would fatten him up so I felt better about myself.

I have a new favorite pair of fat pants but I'm not planning on saying anything to my other pants. I just hope they don't notice. Trips to the closet may get awkward.

I am trying to cut out or eliminate carbs, but this patch of a French baguette taped to my arm isn't working worth a damn.

I'm trying to be more empathetic. Tonight, I said "thank you" to a box of Hamburger Helper.

I was pretty good looking in high school and college. Then I discovered Pop Tarts.

Dieting is easy. Easy as pie. A piece of cake. Crap! No wonder I'm still fat.

My doctor told me that I needed to cut out most refined sugar, carbs and anything high in sodium. I'm also trying to eliminate the majority of meat. Looks like I'll be cornering the market on celery and ice cubes.

I haven't eaten any meat for 10 days. So far, so good, although my faux leather steering wheel cover is starting to look like the most delicious beef jerky ever.

I like to weigh myself naked, but it's always an awkward few moments for the scale.

The other day, I bought an XL t-shirt that was made in China. I don't know what guy the Chinese are using to figure out how big an XL t-shirt should be, but if the one I bought is any indication, it's me at 12-years-old.

I know that a couple of my New Year's resolutions are going to be lose weight and get some color; I look like a giant, soft pretzel that's been left out in the rain.

Facebook, Computers and Technology, Oh My

The vast majority of things I have written here are things that I have posted on Facebook. Hey, when you have over 100 friends (you read that right, OVER 100!) there is pressure to perform. Sometimes I get three or four 'likes' from one posting (Yes, again you read that correctly). I used to have a Twitter account, but I realized it wasn't just to send electronic Haiku messages and it lost all of its coolness for me.

I don't want my computer to reproduce, but I'm worried because it relies on the algorithm method.

My password made me so mad I was going to take it to court, but I didn't because it's case sensitive.

Dear computers, please stop asking me if I'm human; I never ask if you're toaster ovens. Thanks.

It's not my fault. My algorithm made me do it.

If you like my Facebook posts, you agree that I can access your public profile, friend list, dental records, current city, baby pictures, birthday, the video you made with your last "special friend," personal descriptions, social security number, likes and your friends' interests, that key under the mat, photos you have posted, footage from your appearance on *Cops*, songs you have listened to or shared, images from your toenail fungus removal procedure and the size of any recently purchased undergarments.

I really want to download and play Pokémon Go, but I can't leave my Tamagotchi alone.

So, this is how tired I was when I came home from work today. I walked through the door and thought, "I should probably check my messages." Good grief.

I went on Yelp to rate Polaris of the constellation Ursa Minor. I gave it one star.

Little, portable memory storing devices were originally called thumb drives, then opposable thumb drives and are now known as flash drives. That's evolution.

Remember when we had AOL dial-up in the late 90's and would wait patiently for that super-cute image of ten frisky kittens in a basket to appear? Or we would wash the car while we waited to download that short video of a skateboarding teen leaving his testicles behind when he attempted the slide-down-the-handrail trick? Now, if takes more than a nanosecond for us to start streaming that nine-hour video on the nesting habits of the arctic loon or download the complete works of Salvador Dali in 3-D, we freak out.

Texting is my upper body workout.

I just spelled a word so wrong, autocorrect laughed in my face and took the rest of the day off.

I went to the online school of hard knocks.

What's up with Yelp? I just wrote a review for a gym I'm going to and Yelp wants to know if there's a PokéStop nearby! Hey, unless I see Pikachu on a Stairmaster, I don't care.

FACEBOOK, COMPUTERS AND TECHNOLOGY, OH MY

Finally figured out how to install Auto-Tune in the shower. I sound great in there now! Check for dates of my upcoming concerts.

So, I have divided the group of "people you may know" that Facebook offers up into 4 basic categories:

1. People who I do indeed know but want to be friends with about as badly as I want to remove my own wisdom teeth.
2. People who I may have heard something vague about either through friends, via restroom graffiti or on a third world infomercial.
3. People who I have no clue about and who are clearly friends of friends or family seven times removed or in prison.
4. Imaginary friends, cartoon characters and Kevin Bacon.

Looks like in my new apartment, I have to choose between Comcast and AT&T. That's like asking me which I would rather have, a huge pus-filled abscess or the worst case of jock itch ever.

My apartment has a hard-wired smoke alarm or, as I like to call it, "HEY! I THINK THE TOAST IS DONE!"

I took the road less traveled because my GPS told me to.

I want to call tech support for my computer and tell them I haven't been able to use my computer for two days because I need the cursor to go just a little further to the right, but my mouse is right at the very edge of the mouse pad! Help!

I just read something interesting. In a new study, researchers found that rats exposed to cell phones were more likely to develop cancer. As part of the same study, researchers weren't surprised to find that rats calling any cell phone customer service center were more likely to kill themselves immediately.

I wanted to keep an image on my desktop from re-populating, so I used the snipping tool.

I just imaginary peed into a waterless urinal. Wow. Technology.

People who only post pictures of themselves that they take themselves in their bathroom when they are by themselves really (really) need to get out more and make some friends. MAYBE A FRIEND WITH A CAMERA OR A SKETCH PAD AND A SHARPENED #2.

You can never be too rich, too thin or have too many flash drives...

It's sad when you add a new phone number to your cell phone just so you know not to answer when that person calls.

I cut my cable service to next-to-nothing because I knew I could get by with Netflix, Hulu Plus and our Roku devices. But when Comcast said I would be getting minimal programming and some obscure channels, I didn't know that they would include such gems as: The Ginsu Knife Channel (one infomercial from the 1970s played over and over again. If you added some Michael Bolton music in the background, it would be the Hell on Earth Channel); The All-Girl Scandinavian Debate Channel features tall, leggy blondes with names like Ingrid and Petronella talking about the relative merits of a market-based economy versus a centrally controlled economy (Note: I actually watch this one); Hermit Crab Fight Club! This involves staged fights between trained hermit crabs. Unfortunately, as the hermit crabs don't actually fight, it is fair to say that the tension is not palpable.

FACEBOOK, COMPUTERS AND TECHNOLOGY, OH MY

I have never killed an inanimate object before, but I'm about to put my wireless router in a massive chokehold and squeeze until the two crappy signal bars slowly fade away and flat line. Then, there will be nothing left but the memory of me standing on our bed and leaning way to the left to just to get Netflix on my Kindle.

Some guy in Missouri conned women into buying him luxury cars, (Lamborghini, Cadillac Escalade and Corvette) in a scam he perfected using the "Plenty of Fish" dating app. I thought that if he could do it, so could I. Unfortunately, my attempts did not work out as well, but if anyone needs a can opener, half a box of expired Girl Scout cookies or a Chia Pet, I can hook you up.

It's official. I now have more flash drives than toes.

Groupon really, really wants me to have a colonoscopy.

When you go to the movies now, the announcements they make asking people not to use their cell phones are really clever. I like to record them.

I can now speak sarcasm flawlessly, without even a hint of an accent. Thank you, Rosetta Stone.

When someone sends me an e-mail written in Times New Roman, I respond with an e-mail written in Wingdings. Tit for tat.

Someone just liked a comment I made on Facebook eight years ago. Fire up the DeLorean!

Recently, my life passed before my eyes, but I didn't have to watch it with commercials because I have TiVo.

I just realized for the first time, I have 40 followers on Facebook. I don't know any of them. I've always kind of sensed there was someone behind me. Electronically.

My Internet connect has been spotty, so if I can't get online, please just call me and tell me what the cute kittens in the box are doing.

My cell phone is starting to show its age. It's slow, the memory's full and I can't add anything new. Yes, we have a lot in common.

Nobody calls anymore. Everyone is either texting or IMing. When my phone rings, my mind immediately makes a short list of people I know who might be dead.

I wouldn't want to live in Wyoming. I'm sure it's nice, but I would develop a complex having to scroll to the last state on the drop down every single time I filled anything out online.

I think before you get serious about someone, you need to spend a couple of days with that person somewhere with no Wi-Fi and no cell phone reception to see what they are really like.

You know you're staying up too late when you nod off while watching Netflix and drop your Kindle on your face.

I've been checking Craigslist for some sort of time portal that will allow me to show up at work in the morning and fast forward through the time-space continuum to the end of the day. So far no luck, but one guy did say he had a riding mower with no reverse so...you know...getting there.

I ordered the Rosetta Stone levels one, two and three "HOW TO SPEAK IN ALL CAPS" language course. I still need to work

FACEBOOK, COMPUTERS AND TECHNOLOGY, OH MY

on the exclamation points, but other than that, SO FAR SO GOOD!!

Why does spell check sometimes work on Facebook, and other times it doesn't? Inquiring minds want to know.

I'm changing my relationship status with my snooze button to, "It's complicated."

Sometimes I make a less-than-legal U-turn just to show my GPS that I'm in charge.

Lacolikaphobia: the fear of getting no likes on your super witty Facebook posts.

I'm getting a little tired of the GPS on my phone. It's always the same thing; "Turn right in 100 feet," "Make a U-turn when safe" and "You are approaching your destination". It's accurate, but just a little boring. I think your GPS should sound more like your significant other, occasionally throwing in a line that we've all heard before:

"Are you sure this is the right way?"

"Why don't we pull over and ask someone?"

"You have no idea where we are, do you?"

"Good God, I just know that we are going to end up in the *Children of the Corn* cornfield!"

My cell phone wasn't obeying my voice commands, so I had to swat it with a newspaper.

I downloaded some software, and when I registered it I realized something. The United States is no longer number one in the world. I don't mean in terms of military might or gross national product. I mean that on the scrolling drop-down lists you have to complete to fill out a form or register a product, the United States is number 244 out of 257. Now I am all for being politically correct, but if you're downloading American software from an American company in America, is it really necessary that one leapfrog over Andorra, Lesotho and the Paracel Islands to get to the United States? No human beings reside on Bouvet Island (the environment is too harsh) but they are number 32 on the list, 212 spots ahead of the U.S. Yes, I will admit it, it does bother me that some lichen and moss have beaten us just because they are alphabetically superior. I'm trying not to sound like a homer for all things Americana, but it's hard when the United States barely (barely!) beats out the likes of Vanuatu and Wake Island on this thing. I don't know this for a fact, but I'm pretty sure someone in Toga is laughing like crazy at our expense.

My wireless mouse is dying. I literally just called my cursor a bad name—I guess that makes me a cursor, too.

Woke up this morning with the worst allergies I've had in a long time, so tonight I'm going to fire up Netflix to watch the movie "What to Expectorate When You're Expectorating."

Yes, if you push really, really hard on a remote button it will make those dead batteries come to life. Really.

When my neighbors moved, they gave me a very cool Roomba vacuum. Sadly, every time I start it up I feel compelled to yell, "Let's get ready to Roomba!"

In the future, when our human-like androids are perusing the Internet, it's going to be awkward when they get to a website that asks them to check a box that says, "I am not a robot."

I have a hard-wired, burnt popcorn detector that works a little too well.

FACEBOOK, COMPUTERS AND TECHNOLOGY, OH MY

A little tip for everyone out there: if you are like me and wake up in the morning with a moderate to acute need to use the bathroom, the ambient "Babbling Brook" sound on your clock radio may not be the best alarm to use.

I like to do whatever I can do in the evening to help get me ready for the next day. That's why I hit the snooze button 4 or 5 times in a preemptive strike.

I'm not sure how I'm supposed to react when Facebook announces that a friend is nearby. I mean, I'm not going to run out and look for them. Unless of course they are driving an ice-cream truck. That would change everything.

Our electricity went out at work and when it came back on the clock on my PC said September 9, 2013. I took advantage of this lapse in the time-space continuum and purchased a lot of Facebook stock. Lunch is on me. Let's do the time warp again...

As I write this, it's pouring rain and really windy. They say that there's a pretty good chance that the powe

The numbers on the dials of the toaster have completely rubbed off, so you never know what setting it's on. You're either making breakfast or condemning an innocent bagel to death.

This morning my doorbell rang, but when I opened the door nobody was there. Then it happened again. Then it started happening every few seconds. I finally realized that all of the rain was somehow causing the doorbell to short and make it ring on its own. For a while, I thought that every imaginary friend I had ever had was coming to visit at the same time.

No electricity at my place. The lights aren't on, but somebody's home.

I don't know how it's possible, but I'm able to time travel. I sit down at my computer to check a couple of e-mails and then—BAM!!--suddenly I look up and I've been transported 2 or 3 hours into the future!

Computer scientists don't dance well unless they've got a pretty good algorithm.

Sometimes I think my life revolves around keeping things fully charged and not inadvertently wearing the same pair of underwear two days in a row. Both are equally hard, by the way.

This is my horoscope for today: "Capricorn (Dec. 22-Jan. 19) This is a passionate, sexy, romantic day. You want to have fun with your main squeeze. Flirtations will be intense as well." Hmmm…I guess I'm making out with the Roku remote.

Randomness

In a million years, cockroaches will finally be extinct, but Pop Tarts will have survived.

I have a sedentary lifestyle but an overactive bladder so, you know, pretty good balance.

My new favorite headline: "Man's prosthetic eye falls out during trial, judge declares mistrial." OK, cue justice is blind joke here...

When did deodorant get so expensive? I mean $4 or $5 a pop? Really? I may opt for the spend-less-and-be-slightly-stinky option.

The police shut down a local massage parlor last night. Apparently, one of the employees rubbed someone the wrong way.

Online dating has really improved my results. Before, I was getting turned down one or two times a month. Now I can get turned down 8 or 10 times a week!

Five minutes to vacuum, plus fifteen more minutes to figure out how to put all of the attachments back on.

Some people practice noodling, that's fishing for catfish using your bare hands and one arm. I'm not into that, but I kind of go after nose hair the same way.

I think the new maintenance people in our building must be European. The toilets are flushing counter-clockwise.

A rich person sees a quarter on the sidewalk and keeps walking. A normal person picks it up and thinks, "Cool. I found a quarter," and forgets about it. I find a quarter and it's "THIS IS SEVEN MINUTES OF DRYER TIME AT THE LAUNDROMAT! SCORE! YES!"

Whenever I want to feel better about myself, I head on over to the "Faces of Meth – Before and After Photos" website.

"Giant Goat Cheese Fire Closes Norwegian Roadway for Six Days." This is my new favorite headline.

Is it just me, or is there something slightly Medieval and sinister about the name "Black Forest Ham?"

Some things in life are not important. However, understanding and appreciating the difference between a dangling participle and an undescended testicle is critical.

I want a font that says, "I'm pissed off, but I'm dealing with it."

We can put a man on the moon, but we can't make a squeeze bottle of mustard that doesn't dribble out that yellowish, watery stuff no matter how much you shake it.

The Times New Roman font bothers me. There, I've said it.

I hate it when you mangle a word so badly that not even spell checker recognizes it. Then you have to rewrite it, making it slightly less horrible each time, hoping that spell checker finally figures out what the heck you were trying to write.

It really bothers me that people who send spam can't spell better and lack a grasp of basic grammar. I blame the Nigerian school system.

RANDOMNESS

On January 23rd, it's going to be the Chinese Year of the Dragon, but if you're like me, it will take you 2 months to stop writing "Year of the Snake" on your checks.

I'm sorry but I'm fed up with generic, boring fortune cookie fortunes. Panda Express may be feeding my stomach, but they're not doing a thing for my yearning for intellectual enlightenment and my need to have the secrets of the universe spelled out for me on a little piece of paper in 50 characters or less (Wait a minute! Holy crap, the Chinese invented Twitter!).

I started out as a morning person. Then, after a long time, I became a night owl. Now I would love to spend more time just lounging around in bed, but my alarm clock does not care about my happiness.

A little tip for everyone out there. If you're like me and wake up in the morning with a moderate to acute need to use the bathroom, the ambient "Babbling Brook" sound on your clock radio may not be the best alarm to use.

According to scientists studying Chilean earthquakes, the Earth has been permanently deformed by huge quakes. But please, try not to stare because that's really impolite.

Why is it that 72 hotel room degrees feels like 98 regular degrees?

In a fill-in-the-bubble world, I'm kind of a none-of-the-above type of person.

I came home today to a summons for jury duty. I'm already thinking of my excuses to get out of it.

"You guys are cool with no pants Wednesdays, right?"

"I can do it, but I'll need to bring my emotional support emu."

"That's the week I'm supposed to be helping a friend move a couple of bodies, but whatever."

"I don't care who it is or what they did, I'm sending them to prison. I need a new pen pal."

"Is it OK if I binge watch episodes of 'Cops' while deliberating?"

"I believe everyone is guilty until they pay me off."

"Can I please be the jury foreman? I'm updating my resume and I need more special skills."

"What a great opportunity to show off my close-up magic!"

"Hey judge! Do you believe in love at first sight? Because I do now!"

You know those magnifying mirrors that makes a pore on your nose look like a hot tub, and a zit look like Mount Doom? I will NEVER look in one again on an empty stomach.

San Francisco, arguably the most liberal city in the U.S., has banned nudity in public. Another case of the not-very-good-looking naked people ruining it for everyone else!

Apparently, Bangladesh is the largest country to have never won a medal at the Olympics. I'm fairly certain that will change now that the entirely new event of "12-year-old-girls-sitting-on-concrete-factory-floors-knitting-sweaters-for-rich-Americans" has been introduced. Go Bangladesh, go!

I want the super power of knowing the really intimate details about people that will embarrass them the most. "Oh, yeah? Say what you want, but I'm not the guy who wet my pants on that eighth-grade field trip!"

RANDOMNESS

This is terrible, but today, I was talking to a guy who had a blackhead the size of a seedless grape, and all I could think about was getting him in a headlock and popping the hell out of that thing. What is wrong with me?

I'm going to start living more dangerously – only looking one way when I cross the street, only chewing each bite eleven times, getting stuck toast out of the toaster with a fork. You know, crazy stuff like that.

I am writing an erotic novel about a well-to-do stud horse and a young, inexperienced filly called *50 Bales of Hay*.

If I were really rich, I would develop a subdivision of homes just so that I could name the streets. I would give them all really awful names, like Hump a Camel Court, Ass Wipe Circle, Peeling Scab Street, etc. Then, I would make the homes so cheap that people would buy them despite the terrible names. The best part would be when I ran into them as a total stranger and struck up a conversation. "So, where do you live? Huh! What? You're kidding, right? That's the name of your street? Oh my God, what mental degenerate thought of that?"

In our high school play, I played Romeo. I knew it wasn't going well when Juliet leaned over and whispered, "I wish you were really dead."

I bought a loaf of French bread at the store tonight. When I was at the cash register the young lady who was bagging said, "You know, if you ask in the bakery they will slice that for you." I replied, "I have a bread knife at home and a very particular set of skills—skills I have acquired over a very long career of bread cutting." She didn't get it.

Sometimes, as we make our lives, we forget the "stir occasionally" part.

I want to be a back-seat driver in a bumper card, so I can yell, "Come on you sissy! Ram them! Ram them! Turn the wheel the other way!"

I had a dentist appointment this morning. Apparently, I need a deep cleaning, a crown and $840. No, not in that order.

I finally used up and had to throw away my shaving cream for sensitive skin. Yeah, I cried a little.

I told myself that I was going to bed early tonight, but I didn't. So yes, I basically just lied to myself. That's it. I'm breaking it off.

I feel sorry for chickens born without bones in their wings. They only have one contribution they can make to give their lives meaning, and that's to give us something to eat while watching football.

I finally found my Zen. It was under the cushions of my sofa, along with $1.74 in change and a mint from 2013.

I'm not sure how, but after the weekend, I ended up with a wallet full of one-dollar bills. I guess if I'm shipwrecked on a deserted island with nothing but a vending machine and a stripper, I'll be OK.

When I see an ad for something and it says "$500 off!", I know immediately that I can't afford it, even without ever seeing the price. When I see "Save $3 today!" I know it's right in my wheelhouse.

May 7th is World Naked Gardening Day. Please be careful in the handling of your secateurs.

RANDOMNESS

I just read an article called, "10 Troubling Habits of Chronically Unhappy People." It made me mad and filled me with self-loathing.

I completed my bracket and hung three shelves. I was disappointed not to get to the final fourth.

I have made a number of bad decisions in my life. Number 672: over-watering my succulents.

I'm not really smart enough to have low self-esteem issues.

Today is the first day of the rest of your life. Unless you are a Mayfly, in which case you've been screwed since noon.

I was driving today with Riley when she spotted a cat on top of a wooden fence, looking at one side and then the other as if trying to determine the best place to jump down. Riley said, "Dad, that cat is literally on the fence." Smart kid.

That moment, the morning after a Daylight savings time change, when you jump up and shout, "OH CRAP!" because you needed to spring forward an hour ago.

Little tip for you kids who will be going to the dentist soon - don't do what I did. When my dentist was performing the exam and poking and probing inside my mouth and reading off all of those numbers I kept trying to say "Bingo!" He was not amused.

I was with the girls yesterday and we drove by a Men's Wearhouse store. Riley looked at me and asked, "Do they even allow girls in there?"

I'm testing a theory that if you drive the wrong way through a Mexican fast food drive-thru, you can only get fried beans.

Famous Last Words

I went through a period when I gave a lot of thought to the last words I would ever say before kicking the bucket. I realize that I probably don't have a choice in the matter, but I don't want the nasty rumor circulating around at my memorial service that I left this world after stating, "Hey everyone, look at this bucket! I wonder how far I can kick it?"

I've started compiling a list of what I DON'T want my last words to be. Too much time on my hands? Maybe. Here are the first five:

1. Old chainsaws really are the best!
2. Can you believe a brand-new Xbox for $50? I'm meeting this guy I found on Craigslist...
3. Hey buddy! Why don't you pick on someone your own size!
4. This is my 15th Red Bull, and, honest to God, I still don't feel a thing!
5. I had no idea you could buy black market lunch meat!

Here are the next five:

1. Chupacabra? No, that's just some kind of weird-looking dog...
2. Sure, a plunger will work, but let me show you how I like to do it.
3. I just got the KIA tuned up; get ready to feel the power.

4. Is it the black or the red cable that's the ground? In this rain, I can barely tell them apart...
5. Just to be sure I have this noodling thing down, I catch the fish by letting it swallow my arm, right?

Here are the next five:

1. So if I buy two extra-large meat lover's pizzas, I get the third one free? Really?
2. OK, I'll stand here, but don't take the picture until there's a really big wave behind me.
3. Interesting fact: the guy who makes the blowfish sushi here is an ex-con.
4. Directions? Check. Snacks for the trip? Check. Full gas tank in the old Pinto? Check...
5. Hey! Check this out. I just bought a diet book by the doctor who killed Michael Jackson!

And a bunch more:

1. Something smells really, really weird in here.
2. Ten to one I can still fit in these jeans!
3. I'm pretty sure that mayonnaise lasts at least 5 years.
4. Why does the voice on my GPS suddenly sound weird?
5. I can almost reach it...almost...just a little further...
6. They say to turn off the computer before replacing the RAM, but whatever...
7. Oh my God! Look at those cute little bear cubs! Poor babies are all alone.
8. This black-market Viagra doesn't work as well, but you can't beat the price.
9. There's no way this door will open while the plane is in flight, right?

10. Those damn gang bangers next door are so loud! I'll take care of that.
11. Weird...I keep getting these messages, but I don't know anyone on Skype named Rat Man.
12. Wow! Look at all the trucks parked in front of that diner! It must be an awesome place to eat.
13. This new Dyson hand dryer is not only great for drying your hands. Check this out...
14. I'm just heading over to the Mitt Romney stump speech to freak them out with my Obama t-shirt. Ha!
15. I swear to God that the sea monkeys are flipping me off. Really!
16. We cancelled the party, so I'm stuck eating, like, 12 pounds of cheese dip.
17. LOL! I'm texting you from the carpool lane right now!
18. I don't care how gross this restroom is. I'm using it, and I'm not coming out until I'm done!
19. If the friggin' automatic pin reset doesn't work, I'll just crawl in there and get those pins unstuck myself!

Getting Older

I'm not obsessed with getting older, and even though the time machine I ordered from Hong Kong turned out to be a bread maker (my God, that was the worst translation ever) I'm still not sweating my march forward to adult diapers and thinking my girlfriend is some lady from the Welcome Wagon.

I'm feeling really old, like 7 or 8 in underwear years.

Fridays between 4:00 and 5:00 PM, my productivity drops to three-toed sloth on sedatives level. It took me 10 minutes to type this.

Getting old sucks. Yesterday, just walking to my car, I pulled a muscle in my shin. What's next? Dislocate my shoulder by lifting the remote? Cause internal bleeding on the brain by doing long division? Become a leper by putting my toilet seat down? (OK, in fairness, that last one will never happen). Come on, man!

I'm re-growing celery. My hair, sadly, is not getting the hint.

It's official, my brain is full. In order to save a new memory, I have to overwrite an old memory, thus erasing the original file.

My right hip is shot. Scratching Olympic high hurdles off of my bucket list.

I need to go to the eye doctor. My hindsight is only about 20/100.

Ten seconds after I turned 50, I started getting mail from the AARP. They are relentless in their efforts to have me join and are constantly reminding me of the savings an AARP membership brings for things like burial arrangements, oversized rectal thermometers, hearing aids and adult diapers. Seriously, I get something in the mail from them at least 2 or 3 times a week. You would think the AARP would be run by kindly, silver-haired folks who like to sit around and reminisce about the times when gas cost a nickel per gallon and you could have someone killed by a gangster for half a cheese sandwich. But no, oh no. Apparently, it is run like a Glengarry Glen Ross senior center, and someone keeps shouting, "Get that bastard Waldrep! Sign him up! Seal the deal!"

Two of the top trending searches on the internet today were "Grandparents' Day" and "Bladder Infections." I'm not saying they are related, but I did drink a huge glass of cranberry juice after I got home today from meeting up with the girls' grandfather just in case.

Sometimes, when people get older, they need both an actual and a metaphorical hip replacement.

One minute, everything is going along great, and the next minute, you wake up to find you have an ear hair long enough to use as a high wire across Niagara Falls. What the hell?

My eyebrows are starting to look like something out of a Salvador Dalí painting, and not one of the good ones.

When I die I'm going to donate my body to science, but only the good parts.

Pinterest thought I might be interested in following the topic "Hair Beauty." Oh Pinterest, silly Pinterest; unless it involves a comb-over on my back, I'm afraid you're barking up the wrong follicles.

You know your underwear is too old when you can count the rings.

I recently had to do some physical therapy. It hurt like hell. I told the therapist that next time we were only doing metaphysical therapy. He had to think about it.

My front lawn is just like my body: I got stuff growing everywhere except where I want it.

Sometimes I think wouldn't it be great, knowing what I know now, to go back in time to high school? Then I remember algebra class.

I did a good deed and signed up to donate my organs. I mean, what am I going to do with a Wurlitzer after I'm dead?

In car years, I'm in my late 20's, and apparently way overdue for my 120,000 mile major service.

Oh, the car blinker! Used to indicate a right turn, a left turn or a merge into traffic. Also, if left on long enough, a pretty good indicator that someone is well into the AARP age bracket.

Has anyone actually died kicking a bucket?

You know you are getting older when you are trying to hold on for that rest area twenty miles down the road, but your bladder keeps tugging on your shirt sleeve and saying, "Are we there yet?"

It's not having two kids in college, remembering the pet rock craze or the fact that I voted for Jimmy Carter that makes me feel old. It's how far I have to scroll to find my birth year every time I fill anything out a form on the internet!

A nurse just called to schedule my first-ever colonoscopy. Apparently, I'm at the age where it's a good idea to occasionally shove a rubber broomstick with a camera on it up my ass and put the smack down on my colon until it gives up the goods. What goods? I don't know. Maybe it's been withholding information about my small intestine harboring a fugitive hamburger for the past five years. Maybe my colon has turned into public housing for polyps, and it's cramming them in there like drunk college students in a phone booth (I know, I know...what's a phone booth?). At the end of the conversation, the nurse did ask me if I had any questions.

"Just a comment," I said. "I lost a mini-Beanie Baby in 1998, so while you guys are in there doing the Roto-Rooter thing, maybe you can just take a peek for me."

"A Beanie Baby?" she responds, puzzled.

"Yeah, well, I wouldn't ask except that it's collectible. You know..." Silence on the other end of the line. Now, I've got her. "And," I add, "what about any spare change you might find? I get to keep that, right? You guys don't divvy that up while I'm knocked out and butt naked, right?"

"Change?" she asks softly.

"And what about the rights to the video?" I ask. "I mean, you guys are rolling while we all take this mystical journey up my ass's dryer vent, right? I'm not going to wake up and have some kinky video of my internal junk on YouTube, am I?"

"YouTube? What do you mean, YouTube?" she asks.

"Listen," I say, "you're right. Let's cross that anal passage when we get to it."

So, we say our goodbyes. I'm pretty sure my chart has now been flagged. That's OK. When I go in for the colonoscopy, just before they put me under, I'm going to tell the doctor that I knew I was supposed to eat lightly and then fast right before the procedure, but that week-old tuna casserole wasn't going to eat itself when I woke up that morning.

What is going on with my bladder? My bladder used to be the size of a Coleman cooler. Honestly. When I was younger, I could take in and hold more water weight than a pregnant, two-hump camel. I was a human wading pool. I once drove 16 hours straight from Washington State to Northern California consuming, along the way, 12 bottles of water, 10 cans of soda and a bottle of healthy tea that I bought by mistake. Did I stop and pee along the way? No. I held it like a man and didn't even have to start clenching until the last 100 miles (the last 20 minutes, I admit to doing the crazy-leg, Mexican hat dance in the car...not recommended). When I finally let loose, I peed for about two hours straight, making me somewhat of a hero among truck drivers, race horses and (I'm pretty sure) volunteer firemen. Today, my bladder is about the size of a dried lentil. If I back out of my driveway in the morning and there's condensation on the windshield, I have to run back inside to go to the bathroom. If I'm driving, the minute I twist open the top of a bottle of water, my brain sends a signal to my urinary tract to start doing the Macarena, and I'm looking for a place to pull over and try my luck on the urinal bull's eye. If I get a soda at a fast food drive-thru, the second I take the paper off the straw, I have to park and actually go into the fast food place, which very much defeats the purpose. If I'm driving along and, God forbid, the songs "Smoke on the

Water," "Bridge over Troubled Water" or "Madman across the Water" comes on the radio, I get an immediate, cringeworthy urge to go. And sometimes, when I'm driving through a forest and I really don't have to go, I'll still pull over, walk into the woods and let loose. Of course, that has more to do with being a guy and just digging the fact that I can pee on a tree than having a bladder the size of a sea monkey. I'd love to keep writing, but I gotta go.

I still have my wisdom teeth, and lately, they have been doing their best to push through. I don't really feel that much wiser, but I signed up to re-take the SATs just in case.

I think I pulled a hamstring making oatmeal this morning. Translation: I might be on the DL for a couple of weeks for the saddest reason ever.

I don't really mind kids blasting their music at gas stations or convenience stores. I think that kids of every generation have done that (although, blasting Bachman Turner Overdrive on my 8-track with my tiny car speakers didn't exactly cause the windows to shake). I think I'm going to get a new sound system with massive speakers and a roof-mounted woofer and start blasting "Muskrat Love' by the Captain and Tennille. I think that would make a bunch of teenagers freak out and start clawing at their ears. Oh, middle-age payback is sweet!

So, driving to Reno today, I realized that I had left my right blinker on for like 10 miles. Christ, it's starting!

I hadn't realized this until recently, but apparently, when Mr. Magoo died, I inherited his eyebrows.

I'm wondering how old a guy has to be before he can join the "Men Wearing Plaid Shorts, Black Shoes, and White Athletic Socks Club?" I think I would really rock that look.

GETTING OLDER

The older I get, the worse my hearing becomes. I can still, however, hear a kid yell "daddy" from a mile away.

I know I'm too old to say that I'm middle-aged, but I'm using some rollover years that I never activated.

My human odometer will roll over to 60 in December. That seems old, but those are mostly all freeway years so, you know...

Hey everybody! Today is the oldest you've ever been! Congratulations!

I wonder if my high school is going to have a 50-year reunion. I'm not sure I would go, but I'm trying to figure out how long I need to live just in case.

I'm like that pen you carry around in your car; I'm old, leaky and only work at certain angles.

I don't have a bad back, just a back that's been hanging out with the wrong crowd.

I guess if Ponce de Leon were around today, he would be searching for the drinking fountain of youth.

I really don't mind not having hair, but it does make it just a little bit harder to tell if I'm upside down.

The days of the week on my pill dispenser, for the first time in months, are aligned with the actual days of the week! The OCD part of me just did a little happy dance.

It's official: my eyebrows have broken a number of protocols of the Geneva Convention. Next stop, The Hague.

50 is the new 40. 65 is the new 50. Dead is the new slowing down a little bit.

Sometimes I take a power nap for like, 2 or 3 hours. Hey, I'm old and need all the power I can get.

I think I just dislocated my elbow while shaving my head. My baldness is hereditary, so it looks like I'm going to have to sue my own father for damages. Awkward.

You know you're getting older when you start grooving to the elevator music.

I'm finding that the older I get, the further away my car ends up from the spot I parked in.

All day I've been lethargic, with the energy of a three-toed sloth. Now, nearing midnight, I'm wide awake, energized and feeling creative. I should have been a cat burglar, or a jazz musician...or a pimp.

After nearly four years, I just discovered that there is a button on the microwave that conveniently adds 30 seconds to the heating time. Now if you'll excuse me, I'm going to drive around the block two dozen times with my left turn signal on.

The Ford Mustang is 52 years old. I'm a little bit older so it gets all my hand-me-downs.

Why, dear God, would any man wear a toupee? I just can't understand what could cause someone's vanity to slingshot past their common sense to such an extent. Hey, no man likes being bald, and I can tell you that if I didn't have my back hair for moral support, it would be even tougher. But why would any man want to put something on their head that was pieced together by some 12-year-old Chinese girls in the same factory where they make artificial putting greens and industrial strength mops? How do you segue suddenly into just showing up to work one day with some freshly skinned road kill on the top of your previously shiny dome? This is where, "Oh this? I ran into a door," won't cut it as an excuse for your precipitous change into the world's largest Chia Pet. You can spot a toupee a mile away. I won't even say a "bad toupee" because that's so incredibly redundant that if I say it, it will come back up my throat in the middle of the night like excessive verbal reflux. Wearing a toupee is not unlike wearing a Christmas sweater in August that is two sizes too small and inside out. It screams out to be noticed, but you can't politely point out the obvious. You just have to avert your eyes, press your lips together and do what you have to in order to suppress your gag reflex. The trouble with Tribbles is not that they multiplied ad nauseam on the Star Trek Enterprise, but rather you killed one and stapled it to your head.

I'm the hair not apparent of a long line of bald men.

I'm not old. I'm a collectible.

Travel

I travel quite a bit for my job. After not making it in stand-up comedy, as the lead singer of a rock band or as a professional basketball player, I navigated to the next logical choice...retail. Here are a few of my observations and mostly true accounts from my travels. All aboard! (That's a poor choice of words as not one of these anecdotes takes place on a train. I apologize profusely. I really feel terrible now).

I just played my favorite computer game. It's called: "Get-your-Southwest-boarding-pass-the-SECOND-it-becomes-available-so-you-don't-have-to-sit-in-the-middle-seat-of-the-last-row-between-a-sumo-wrestler-and-a-life-insurance-salesman." That's the long title anyway.

I'm going to be travelling for work for the next three weeks. I'm going to give my fake plants a tear-free and insincere goodbye.

Just boarded my Southwest flight. I was B60, but I don't think I look a day over B45.

On the almost four-hour plane ride from Seattle to Anchorage, the nerdy guy sitting next to me really, really wanted to have a long conversation about all of the Resident Evil games and movies, including what my opinion was about each one and how I would rank them and which ones had the best CGI, etc. I asked him how much he knew about massive genital warts somehow forming in the shapes of former famous presidents' heads, not unlike a little Mt. Rushmore in your underpants. Surprisingly, we did not talk much after that.

The TV in this hotel takes forever to go from one channel to the next. It's like playing an electronic slot machine.

Who decided that you had to have a PhD to figure out how to set the alarm on a hotel clock?

Once I let my mind wander, and it spent two weeks in a hotel in Bakersfield. That's an imaginary mini-bar bill I'll never get back.

You know you're tired when you incorporate the sound of your alarm clock into your dream. "Hey! Why is there a big truck backing up all of a sudden? What's going on, here?"

It's almost 11:30 PM and the people in the hotel room next to me are making a lot noise. Am I going to let it bother me? No. Am I going to call their room at 5:00 AM tomorrow morning and ask then to urgently pick up a letter that was left for them at the front desk? Yes. Yes, I am. Is that letter going to say, "Good morning! It must have been hard getting up after such a late night! Have a great day!" That is a strong possibility.

Just checked into the hotel in Fresno. The room was really hot when I walked in, so I turned on the AC. It immediately started making a loud, annoying, high pitched noise. I waited for a few minutes, but the noise didn't stop, so I called the front desk and explained the problem.

I asked, "Can you either have someone come up and fix it or move me to another room?"

The young lady said that they didn't have a maintenance person available at that moment and that they were somewhat short on rooms.

"What kind of noise is making," she inquired.

I replied, "It's like a howler monkey in heat. It's like an angry banshee in a wind tunnel. It's like feedback on the radio when you are right between the hip-hop station and top country hits. It's like a three-year-old in Toys R Us not getting what he wants. If it were an octave higher, dogs would turn into zombies and attack the hotel."

I stopped and asked her if she got the idea. She gave me another room.

Just went through security at Fairbanks Airport. It was me and seven TSA agents. Not another soul in sight. It took fifteen seconds to get through. I felt like I was sneaking on the best ride at Disneyland in the middle of the night.

So today, as I was driving to Reno, a woman driving a U-Haul moving van almost ran me off the road (and over the side of the mountain) when she tried to get into my lane with me in it. After getting back on the road (and peeing myself ever so slightly), I passed her and just drove on. Ironically, about twenty minutes later, I was at a rest stop talking on the phone when who should pull in? Yes, the U-Haul death dealer. I went up to her and said, "Hey, no biggie, but you almost killed me back there. I'm just saying..."

She replied nonchalantly, "Oh, really? Sorry about that," and that was it. I left. It was the most anti-climactic, near-death, road rage experience ever.

I shouldn't write this while I'm driving, but I finally caught a Pokémon! Yeah! Oh, wait a minute. Never mind, I take that back; I ran over a chipmunk.

Yes! Only 950,246 miles to go to be a Million Miler on my airline card!

I just spent ten minutes looking for my car in a parking lot. Oh yeah, that's right – I'm thousands of miles from home and driving a rental.

Sometimes you don't realize that something has a capacity to shine until things are at their darkest. No, I'm not being poetic. I just happened to notice the glow-in-the-dark TV remote in my hotel room when I turned out the lights.

I dutifully passed through the TSA scanner, assuming the awkward, frozen-in-time, jumping jack position with my feet in the yellow footprints on the mat. Then, I walked out and put my feet, once again, on the yellow footprints, waiting for the crossing guard (I mean super-motivated TSA agent) to give me the thumbs up and let me retrieve my belt, shoes and 11 pounds of loose change from the plastic bin at the end of the conveyor belt. That's when I got the bad news.

"Sir," the TSA agent told me, "I'm afraid we've detected a groin abnormality in your scan." I looked back at the scanner, and, sure enough, my Lego-man, yellow outline of a body had a small, red square smack dab in the general vicinity of tighty-whiteyville.

"Do you think it's the steel plate in my right testicle?" I asked. "Not everyone who served in Occupy Wall Street came back in one piece, buddy."

The TSA agent was not amused. "I'm going to need you to go with these two agents, please," he said, indicating the *Of Mice and Men* pair who had joined the party. I was led into a small room and given a brief explanation of how this was going to go down. I noted immediately the complete and utter lack of enthusiasm the pair seemed to have for the job at hand. The one who seemed to be in charge explained the hilarity that was about to ensue.

"Sir," he said in a flat voice, "because of the result of your scan and the area in question, we are required by law to conduct a search of your, um, well, that area. You will be able to leave your pants on." He clearly was not looking forward to this. "Do you have any questions?"

"No. I get it. You're going to feel me up. Go trout fishing in America. Put your thumb on the scale. Say hello to my little friends. Cast a wide net and haul in your limit of genitalia. Yeah, I get it."

He had no response to this, but just began his (surprisingly gentle) cupping. At this point, my goal was to make him as uncomfortable as possible. So, while he cupped and poked, as if he were trying to determine if a fresh loaf of bread was done, I keep up a steady banter. "You know, we would be legally married in 11 states by now. Am I supposed to be feeling tingly all over? If you want me to cough at any time, just let me know. Do I feel a little uneven to you? I have been told I have a bit of a dangling participial on the right. I don't know if this is a full service pat down, but my inner thigh is a little tight. This is weird, but I'm having a senior prom flashback." And then, thankfully, it was over, and I was on my way. But not without two new, special friends and a pair of underwear sure to evoke memories from that point forward.

OK, in hindsight, it's not a good idea to start a two-hour drive with a couple of high fiber bran muffins and a huge energy drink.

The worst thing about early morning flights: "Hey, isn't this the same (slightly damp) towel I used to dry off four hours ago?"

I'm in the airport in Seattle waiting for my flight to Anchorage. A few seconds ago a young couple sprinted by at almost a full on run, awkwardly lugging their bags, pushing a stroller and clutching their boarding passes like winning lottery tickets. They were both sucking in air like the fat kid in P.E. and the panicked look on their faces said it all: "We are about to miss our flight." In contrast, the little three-year-old in the stroller was so happy, grinning ear-to-ear, waving her arms in the air and practically screaming, "Go faster Mommy! Go faster!" Sometimes life offers you a glimpse of beautiful contrast.

Apparently, the A/C in my hotel room only has two settings: off and full-throttle, freezing, Arctic air, gale force wind storm cold enough to freeze your snot and totally invert your testicles. I'm having a hard time deciding which one to go with.

Judging from the noise coming from the hotel room above me, it seems to be occupied by Thumper, a Mexican wrestler, a couple of Mandrake plants, Charlie Brown's teacher and some guy who made one trip too many to the all-you-can-eat Vindaloo chicken buffet.

The TV in this hotel takes forever to go from one channel to the next. It's like playing an electronic slot machine.

While flying home today there was this guy in the Seattle airport who totally looked like he should be an international assassin. I was very tempted to go up to him and say, "I thought Jason Bourne killed you."

TRAVEL

Note to self: not a good idea for anyone involved to hang out the "do not disturb" sign when naked.

A long time ago, I stayed in a nice hotel. I asked the front desk receptionist to go out, but she said no. I asked one of the housekeepers out, but she also declined. So I guess the reviews for that hotel were true; they really did have excellent turn down service.

Driving back from Fresno yesterday, I got into an ugly fight with my GPS. She said some things that were just wrong. I said some things I later regretted. She is just so stubborn and rigid and unyielding. I like to mix things up once in a while. Anyway, I think we're OK now.

This morning there were, literally, ten cars in a row where the driver was texting while driving. It made me so mad, I almost couldn't finish writing this before I got to work.

I have a new clock app on my Kindle. I got it specifically so I could use my Kindle as a nightstand clock with an alarm that was easier to use than the typical PhD-highly-suggested, IQ of 197 plus required hotel clock radio. Last night, I set the alarm and fell blissfully asleep while the neon green, analog numbers softly bathed the room in a dim glow suitable for a scene in a Ridley Scott Alien movie. I was in a deep sleep when the alarm went off this morning: a loud, slumber-shattering, Pokémon seizure-inducing, high-pitched beeping that is the electronic equivalent of nails on a chalkboard. I shot straight up in bed with one thought and one thought only: *How do I turn this thing off?* In my cheery state of setting the alarm last night, I didn't go so far as to figure that out. Holding my Kindle, each jarring note of the alarm hitting me like a hellish combination of a dentist's drill and a dozen mosquitoes mating in my eardrum, I pushed and slid and swiped everything I could see on the screen to no avail. The alarm continued to warn of impending tsunamis and an imminent German air raid. OH MY GOD, MUST MAKE IT STOP! I tried closing the app, but that didn't work. I opened it again and went into the menu, looking for a way to end the madness, but there was nothing there. SWEET, BLESSED JESUS AND ALL THAT IS HOLY, WHAT DO I HAVE TO DO? I fiddled and fussed and then, as I imagined an angry mob of hotel guests armed with pitchforks, clubs and torches (and maybe a Kindle of their own! Gasp!), it hit me. YOU IDIOT, JUST TURN IT OFF! Pushing down on the power button with enough pressure to stop blood from spurting out of a major artery, and with the alarm from hell still screeching at me like a cheated-on girlfriend, the Kindle greeted me with this screen: "DO YOU WANT TO SHUT DOWN YOUR KINDLE?" followed by two buttons reading "Shut Down" and "Cancel." At that moment, I had never wanted anything so badly in my life. I tapped, tapped, tapped the "Shut Down" button like one of Poe's ravens and watched as the Kindle's screen turned black and, FINALLY, off. BEEP! BEEP! BEEP! WAIT A MINUTE... THE ALARM IS STILL GOING! HOW IS THIS POSSIBLE? Had I downloaded an app from the future? Was my Kindle being run by some demonic creature from Hell? Am I being punked? Did someone just really, really want to make sure I didn't oversleep? I jumped out of bed thinking that I might be able to flush the Kindle down the toilet. That's when I noticed my cell phone on the floor, where I had apparently knocked it to in the middle of the night. OH YEAH, I had set the alarm on my phone as a back-up, just in case, and it was my phone, not my Kindle, that was beeping like R2-D2 high on meth and a bad can of WD-40. I turned off my phone, and the room was once again silence. Oops. My bad. And my Kindle app? It never did turn on the alarm. I'm going back to bed.

TRAVEL

If little Johnny goes on a trip for 7 days and needs one pair of socks and one pair of underwear for each, day how many pairs total does he need of each? I don't know the answer, apparently, because I have 8 pairs of socks and 6 pairs of underwear. This new math is killing me!

Because I've been flying so much for work, I've been elevated in the airlines' caste system from a guy for whom an upgrade was pretty much untouchable to a guy who maybe gets a bump up to first class every three or four flights. That little taste of seventh heaven has really soured me on the cattle car that exists behind the magic curtain. It's not the snob appeal. It's not the somewhat superior food or drink. It's not even the fact that I can get out of the plane 10 seconds after they open the door. No, it's really all about the first-class seat.

Back in coach, the subsidized airline housing for the 98%, some sadist determined that three across seating on either side of the plane with an aisle just wide enough for a fashion model on meth to shimmy through would work out just fine. It hasn't. The three-across seating method makes for a lose-lose flying experience. Let's examine each seat so that I may prove my point.

The window seat: There are some positive things that come with the window seat. Not surprisingly, having a window is one of them. But if you fly a lot, the magic of imagining cumulus clouds as big puffs of cotton and little miniature buildings and cars as, well, little miniature buildings and cars soon wears off. Whenever there is actually something of note to look at (cue your captain telling you to look out the right side of the aircraft to see some mountain, a lake, or the lights of Winnemucca, NV), the person in the middle seat is going to lean over and crane their head to and fro so that they, too, can see whatever wonderfulness is out there. If the exact, questionable scenario were happening in a parked car and a cop went by, you would get a quick burst of white light, a couple seconds of flashing lights and sirens, and a deep voice coming over the PA speaker telling you to 'move along'. The window seat also requires that you have a bladder the size of a bread maker, because when the window seat person needs to get up and go, aisle and middle-seat folks need to dislodge and shuffle over and out like guests on a late-night talk show. Finally, if a Canadian goose makes a wrong turn and become mock foie gras after getting sucked into an engine, you'll be among the first to know and will have a front-row seat to impending disaster. I don't want to be the messenger on that one.

The middle seat: Much like the Susan B. Anthony dollar, the middle seat has virtually no redeeming features. Unless you are a rail-thin contortionist and can fold your shoulders like your expensive headphones, inward and flat against your body, you are going to be uncomfortable. Murphy's Law of the middle seat states that the probability is high you will have a sumo wrestler on one side of you and a big 'ol hillbilly (softly humming "Dueling Banjos" under his breath) on the other. There's nothing worse than spending three hours between the proverbial rock and hard place, unable to exhale fully while your arms are folded high and tight across your chest like an extremely disappointed hall monitor.

The aisle seat: The aisle seat is still my seat of choice despite its many shortcomings. The upside is that I can stand up in the aisle without having to do the funky chicken slide and scoot when coming from the window seat. The down side is really all about that winning hypothesis which states two solid objects cannot occupy the same space. My shoulders are wider than the actual seat, meaning there is always a part of me hanging out there in the aisle that the airline has deemed as fair game. If I had a quarter for every time my shoulder or elbow has been clipped by the corner of the stainless steel beverage cart, I could afford to buy my own upgrades for life. But the worst thing about the aisle seat is when two people going in opposite directions decide to pass each other in the aisle in your general vicinity. What is almost physically impossible can only happen if each of those people protrudes way in towards the seat. That is when you find yourself with a face full of either someone's crotch or someone's ass as those two people make enough physical contact to be considered married in Kentucky.

I watched a flight attendant put a verbal smack down on a kid today, and it was beautiful. As our flight was getting ready to take off, a couple of minutes after the announcement had been made to turn off all electronics, a 20-something-year-old guy in a seat across the aisle was still playing around with his tablet when an older, very sweet-looking flight attendant came our way. When she got to our row she looked over at the young man and said very nicely, "Excuse me, sir, I'm going to need you to turn that off now." Without looking up, the kid muttered, "In a minute" in a tone that any parent would instantly recognize as young people speak for, FOR THE LOVE OF GOD, CAN'T YOU SEE I'M BUSY DOING SOMETHING? PLEASE JUST LEAVE ME ALONE FOR TWO MINUTES WHILE I FINISH THIS THING I'M DOING OF MONUMENTAL IMPORTANCE THAT YOU DON'T EVEN UNDERSTAND, JEEZ, AND OMG, STOP BUGGING ME! The flight attendant smiled and said, "Sir? Sir?" until the kid finally looked up at her. "Turn…that…off…right…now," she said in a tone that would have made Dirty Harry pee his pants, accentuating each word like she was speaking to a naughty two-year-old or a shoe-chewing puppy. The pleasant smile was still there, but the eyes were flinty steel like David Banner's before turning into the Hulk. It was subtle, but it was there. It was awesome. The kid's eyes got big, and his jaw literally dropped, and he froze for a second. If he had been a deer he would have been certain road kill. When he snapped back, he got the tablet turned off in about three seconds. He looked at the flight attendant like a guilty Catholic schoolboy about to get his knuckles smacked on by an industrial-strength ruler. "Thank you," the flight attendant said simply and sweetly before moving on. I wanted to cheer. It was a beautiful thing.

Aside from the carpool lanes and the regular lanes, we need a lane designated "Really Old Men Wearing Hats with the Blinker Still On."

On my way to Las Vegas for three days of meetings and seven minutes of fun. Going through security, I asked the TSA guy if my fruit basket would be affected by the X-ray. "You have a fruit basket in there?" he asked. "No. It was more of a hypothetical question," I said. Hey...I just wanted to leave him with food for thought.

Sitting next to three nuns in the Portland Airport. One has an iPad, one has a laptop, and one has a new smartphone. Is there a God? I'm not sure, but I guess there's an app for that.

The alarm clock in my hotel room didn't work. I called the front desk to see if I could get another one.

Front Desk: Can I help you?

Me: Hey, my alarm clock isn't working. Can I get another one?

Front Desk: Oh. What's wrong with it?

Me: You can't see the numbers.

Front Desk: What numbers?

Me: The numbers that you need to see to actually determine the time. What a minute! Did I get a room for clairvoyants?

Front Desk: For what?

Me: Never mind. So this clock is broken. Can I get another one?

Front Desk: Is it plugged in?

Me: Sweet Jesus! I thought it was powered by hydrogen. Let me check. Yes, it is plugged in.

Front Desk: Did you dim it?

Me: I may have tried to Dim Sum it. Not great. Tasted like chicken.

Front Desk: Chicken?

Me: No, I didn't dim it.

Front Desk: Oh, OK. So, do you want another one?

Me: I'm pretty sure that's why I called.

Front Desk: OK, I'll have someone from housekeeping bring you one in about 10 minutes.

Me: Man, if only I could determine the passing of time to know when 10 minutes have expired.

Front Desk: Sorry?

Me: Me too. Thanks.

I was driving down the freeway today with the windows half open (my A/C stopped working the other day) when I look over and see a wasp the size of a cocktail wiener doing the uptown funk on the inside of the passenger side window. No worries, I think as I push the button to lower the window. He'll just fly out when it's all the way down, right? Wrong. Somehow the physics got all wonky and the man-killing wasp was propelled like a rocket to the right side of my neck. After screaming like a little girl, I grabbed the first thing I could find to defend myself. It happened to be my Kindle, which was charging on the passenger seat. Anyone driving by me at this point would have looked over and seen a guy in a panic, screaming obscenities while beating himself senseless about the head and neck with an electronic reading device. I finally landed a lethal blow, and the demon wasp landed on the passenger seat, feet up and motionless. With a great sense of relief, I continued down the highway, hoping my underwear was slightly damp as a result of sweating in the heat and not as a result of the much less desirable alternative. Suddenly, in the tradition of every slasher movie ever made, the seemingly dead wasp rose up and starting buzzing around the car again. What the hell? WHAT THE HELL? This time, I pulled off the freeway and went mano-a-mano with the little bastard until it was pulp.

DIE, WASP, DIE!!! After a quick victory dance, I was back in the car and on my way with all the windows up.

I don't like to brag, but I lived abroad for 10+ years and have traveled to 20 or so countries. Do you know what that means? I know how to flush a toilet anywhere! Yes!

You know that commercial where people are trying to duplicate the sound their car is making to a mechanic? I've been trying to figure out the clunking noise that was at times, coming from the back of my car. After an extensive check, I was able to make a diagnosis: a can of black olives rolling around in my trunk. I now plan to do a loose, canned goods check every 3,000 miles.

Forget about when the stars align—I'm happy to hit three or four green lights in a row.

When you go to England and want an English muffin, do you just ask for a muffin? If so, then how do you get a regular muffin? Maybe you just walk into a place in England and say, "I'd like one of those muffins you're famous for!" Then your friend would ask for one of the lesser known muffins. Then your other friend would screw everything up by asking for a muffin top, which is clearly an American innovation. Complicated.

A journey of 1,000 miles begins with a single step (and a couple of energy drinks, a full playlist, a bran muffin the size of a toaster and a pretty good idea of how far it is to the first rest stop).

My new bumper sticker reads; "I brake for people who slam on their brakes in front of me for no apparent reason."

Sometimes I want to call the toll-free number I see on the truck or work van in front of me just to say, "Wow! Your driver is driving great! Best driver ever!"

I took my car to get the oil changed. I also told the guy to fully lubricate my gas pedal assembly. I don't think that's something one grown man should ever say to another.

When I was in middle school in the early 1970s, we had to learn the metric system. We were told that soon everything in the United States was going to go metric. Our teacher was most emphatic that if we didn't want to be left behind in the shadow of our European cousins (and no one did), we'd better buckle down and be ready for any number of pop quizzes dealing with Celsius, grams and centimeters. Yesterday I filled up my car in gallons under sunny skies while enjoying a beautiful 72 degree Fahrenheit day. As it turns out, the metric takeover here in America had about as much traction as the Yugo and leg warmers over jeans. Of course if you visit Europe today, you'll still be able to put your knowledge of metrics to good use. In the mid-1980s, I knew that Europe used the metric system. I had, after all, been living in Madrid for nearly two months and was a practicing daily. After a couple of months, I thought I was really getting the hang of the whole metric thing. That, together with my piecemeal Spanish, seemed to be getting me by just fine after some initial bumps in the "Calle."

However, after the first couple months in the capital city of Spain, I figured out that gasoline was not incredibly cheap as I first thought, but rather I was paying per liter and not per gallon (1 gallon is nearly 4 liters). Once I figured out the true price of gas, I was happy to rent the tiny, knees-against-my-chest Fiat Uno. I stopped shopping for long underwear when I was told that the 40 degree Celsius summer days were really 104 degrees in Yankee talk, and my fears of getting a speeding ticket for clocking over 120 on the freeway went away when 120 kilometers per hour worked out to be a keep-up-with-traffic 75 miles per hour. Just as well; that was about the top speed for that little Fiat. I thought my old middle school teacher would have been proud of me. I was feeling quite proud of myself, but then I had what I call "the incident" in the Mercado near the Plaza Major in the center of Madrid.

I had been sent to buy chorizo, a delicious type of Spanish sausage, for a party that my fellow American residencia slummers were going to throw for a couple of visitors from the States. That seemed simple enough. Buy enough chorizo to slice up and put out at a party for 20 or 30 people. I guessed that two or three pounds might be enough. Then I thought I might even get a little extra, as I can eat good chorizo morning, noon or night, and I knew my friends would help themselves as well. So, maybe I would get five pounds. Seemed safe enough. When I got to the stall of the vendor with, in my opinion, the best chorizo in town, I had a sudden and inexplicable case of brain freeze. For some reason the pound to kilo (or vice versa) conversion turned to mush in my brain and I could not remember what-was-what. The tough-as-nails looking woman behind the counter asked me what I wanted.

"Chorizo," I said meekly.

"How much?" she asked in Spanish.

I had a small panic attack. I seemed to remember that either the pound or the kilo was about twice as much as the other. Or was I thinking of something altogether different? A line was forming behind me. My mild panic attack ratcheted up a couple of levels. I took a shot in the dark. I knew I wanted about five pounds. I told her I wanted ten kilos.

"Diez kilos?" she asked, with a look that made me immediately realize that I had backed the wrong horse on the conversion chart in my head. But there was no turning back. I told her yes, yes indeed, I wanted ten kilos of chorizo, hoping the tone in my voice said, *"Don't you think I know what I want?"*

She gave me a funny look and nodded as she began to slice chorizo. And slice. And slice. And slice some more. The little pile of chorizo grew, as did the crowd around the stall. I might've imagined hearing someone mutter something about a crazy American, but I don't think so.

Several minutes later I was walking back to the residencia, lugging a little over twenty-two pounds of chorizo. A kilo, as I've never forgotten, is about 2.2 pounds. I learned a lot during my time in Europe, sometimes at the expense of my pride (and/or digestion system). Now that I have been back in the United States for many years, I sometimes lament the U.S. not adopting the metric system. It seems so much better to say I'm 30 kilos overweight, rather than 65 pounds.

TSA agent: You should remove your belt, otherwise you may be subject to a groin pat down.

Me: Well, I've already had two groin pat downs today, and a third would seem like overkill, so I'll take off my belt.

TSA agent: You've already had two today?

Me: Yes, I have (appropriate pause) Oh! You meant at an airport! Sorry, my bad. No, no pat downs at an airport.

I can't help it. I'm bored.

I fly to L.A. on Thursday. I hope they let me on the plane with my emotional support chupacabra.

More Random Randomness

A postal worker in Florida got busted for running in numerous marathons after going on worker's comp for a back injury. Ironically, her race times actually improved after she went out on her fake claim. Not so ironically, it still takes me 45 minutes at the post office to mail a couple of things and buy a book of stamps.

If I had been born on December 34th, my pin number would be so much easier to remember.

My phone started showing me the weather for Kuala Lumpur for some reason. I didn't realize it at first, and for the past couple of days I was wondering why it wasn't really rainy, in the low 90s and with 87% humidity. I corrected the information on my phone, but now I have a craving for Curry Laksa.

The other day I said something I regretted and had to eat my words. Tasted like chicken.

Whoever thought of using gummies to make adult vitamins is a genius. I never use to get the recommended daily number of vitamins. Now I'm getting 50 to 100 times that amount every, single day! So healthy!

Sometimes when I meet a woman I like I say, "Hey, I know you have to kiss a lot of frogs before you find your prince." Then I ask if I can be one of the frogs.

Why is this string cheese wrapper harder to open than the pain meds I had to take last year for my shoulder? Is America killing itself with opioids AND lactose intolerance?

Unless you're from outer space, please stop using the expression "best of both worlds."

I'm not big on leftover refried beans or, as I call them, re-refried beans.

In this age of processed food which came first, the chicken nugget or the Eggo?

I'm sorry, but your password must contain an uppercase letter, a number, a symbol, a rare blood type, a haiku, a roman numeral and the name of your first pet in Esperanto.

I want to get a dog and name it Karma. That way, when it does something it shouldn't, I can say, "Bad Karma!"

Do you think a rat ever started eating something and then thought, "Whoa! Studies have proven this stuff kills humans!"

Twenty-one people at an event hosted by motivational speaker Tony Robbins suffered second and third degree burns while walking across hot coals, and three of the injured were treated at hospitals. I am now HIGHLY MOTIVATED to never try a stupid stunt like that.

For the first time playing Wii baseball, I hit a Grand Slam AND an out-of-the-park home run in the same game. Sadly, shortly thereafter I was traded for a nunchuk and a Mii to be named later.

I bought a new fridge today. It's not big enough to hide a body or anything, but I can see a tuna casserole getting lost in the back for 3 or 4 weeks.

With the exchange rate, One Direction would be 1.3 Direction in Canada. Not that catchy.

One of the best things about having 6 kids? Virtually unlimited password combinations!

I saw a great bumper sticker today when I was driving. I looked over and saw a stunningly good-looking blonde driving past me in a brand new, red convertible with the top down. As she passed, I saw the bumper sticker which simply read: "You wish." Classic.

Instructions? Instructions? I'm a guy. We don't need any instructions. I like to assemble Ikea furniture in a dark room with butter knife, a tuning fork, a roll of double-sided tape and that wrapper from the chalupa I had for lunch.

One of my New Year's resolutions was to try even harder to pretend I like cats. I just like dogs better, even though I totally don't understand people who get really small dogs. What's the point? When your dog looks like a hamster on performance enhancing drugs, that's just sad (for you and the dog). If you carry around a tiny dog and people mistake it for a keychain, your dog is just too damn small. If you lose your dog in the bottom of your purse between the (curiously strong) tin of Altoids and a pile of Target coupons, then you have a perrito muy chiquito that needs to chow down and bulk up. The only thing that a really small dog is good for is this...you spray them with Pledge furniture polish and slide them under the furniture to collect dust bunnies OR you buy them a tiny saddle and teach a spider monkey to ride. Yippee-ki-yay!

I used to think that Chinese torture methods consisted of slowly dripping water onto a person's forehead, eventually driving the restrained victim insane. But now, I know the truth. The worst form of Chinese torture is untangling miles of made-in-China Christmas lights, spending hours hanging them all up and then finding that one has burned out, making the whole strand useless. TORTURE!

Sitting at the courthouse or DMV, listening to the automated system call out the next number to be served, is like the worst game of Bingo ever.

Strangers are just friends who are now strangers again because you borrowed money from them.

(Please sing to Alanis Morissette's "Ironic")

Took a short trip to the DMV but now they're calling every letter, except the letter B

They're calling H and F and A but that just doesn't jive

Because I'm stuck here in this place until they call B105

And isn't it ironic, don't you think?

When did disposable razors become so expensive? Granted, I use the one with eight blades that vibrates and plays peaceful mood music as I shave, but it seems a shame that my kids are going to have to go to community college on a scholarship because Daddy doesn't want to grow a Unabomber beard.

Five things I'm going to do with my "massive" tax refund:

1. Kids! New shoe laces for everyone!
2. No more discounted three-day-old sushi for a while.
3. Family trip to the mall for a hot dog on a stick and unlimited escalator rides.
4. Inching ever closer to having enough money to make a down payment on a 1987 Yugo.

5. Massive used underwear purchase at the local thrift store.

Well, my "must-do" list for today is shot to hell:

1. I did not use the word "dollop" in a charming or urbane way.
2. I did not have a chance to break the record of the World's Longest Piece of Toilet Paper Stuck to My Shoe event.
3. Finally, I never got around to translating that last chapter of *War and Peace* into one, simple haiku poem. Bummer!

So, what's weird is that a lot of places that take your credit card now just swipe it and hand you a receipt. Quick and easy. But when you use your debit card, you have to navigate through the banking equivalent of the Spanish Inquisition. *Is this the correct amount? Do you want it all on one card? Would you like cash back? Would you like to donate $1 to the Save the Snail Darter Foundation? If you could be any kind of a tree...*

One of the top young Scrabble players in the country has been kicked out of the game's national championship tournament in Florida after he was caught hiding blank letter tiles, organizers said Tuesday. Cheating at a Scrabble tournament? Now, this guy is going to be an outcast to the entire nerd community, shunned by the thick glasses and pocket protector crowd forever, relegated to playing Chutes and Ladders in his mom's basement. Oh, the shame!

I know that I should stick up for the home team (that would be men), but I'm sorry – we are pigs. Thousands of public restrooms attest to this. What is so challenging about directing a stream of urine into a urinal the size of a pygmy elephant from eight inches away without doing the Harlem Shuffle at the same time and swabbing the deck for the next unlucky pee-er? The guy at the state fair, who can flawlessly squirt water into a clown's mouth with laser-like focus, popping his balloon in mere seconds to win a stuffed animal that makes him the envy of every 6-year-old he just beat, is the same guy who pees into a urinal like he's trying to spell his name in the snow. What is the problem, guys? Your penis is not a swizzle stick, and unless it dog-legs like the sixth hole at Augusta, this should be a fairly straightforward operation. I'm sorry, but there is nothing worse than having to mention over the partition to the pee partner on your left that you and he don't have the kind of special relationship that makes it OK for him to splatter your shoes. I don't know what the answer is. Some places have actually put little "bullseye" decals strategically on the inside of urinal. That seems to help. Maybe it's the innate competitive nature of guys that makes many of them channel their inner Robin Hood and attack those bulls-eyes like they are shooting an apple off some restroom attendant's head. Maybe if we could use our strategically placed urine to play Halo or Call of Duty (there's a bad pun there) or Madden, we would never misfire again and hit the floor, the wall or some guy from Madison, Wisconsin. Oh, and don't even get me started on airplane toilets.

Why are people (mostly men) so uptight about the word "vagina?" From the time most guys are about fourteen, the vagina is the holy grail of their existence. Men do incredibly stupid things if they think it will get them just a little bit closer to the magical, mystical, big V. Yet many find the actual word – VAGINA – to be offensive to say. I am going to help the cause. From now on, when saying goodbye to any male friends (OK, not any since I have some friends who are not motivated by any part of the female anatomy), I'm going to say, "See you later! Have a great VAGINA day!" If I don't hear someone clearly, I'm going to say, "I'm sorry...did you say VAGINA?" When I play board games, as soon as someone starts to ask the trivia question like, in the year 1876, who -- I will shout out, "VAGINA!" If I go to a restaurant, I will ask the male server, "So, how's the VAGINA today?" I'm going to start saying to people, "Hey, is that a VAGINA in your pocket or are you just happy to see me?" And on Facebook, I'm going to start asking, "Hey! Where can I click to show that I 'like' that vagina?"

After decades of existence, the United Nations has failed to come up with universal popcorn setting for microwave ovens. What are they doing over there?

You know your underwear is too fancy when it takes you a minute to figure out which way to put them on. I never had this problem with my tighty-whities.

I would rather have a wisdom tooth pulled at the DMV while listening to elevator music than watch reality TV.

These are punchlines. I don't have the actual joke yet, but hey, the hard part is done!

1. Sure, but then you end up with a parrot and a bad haircut!
2. Only once, but in fairness, she didn't see the chandelier.
3. What? I thought you said watermelon on the grass!
4. So, if anything happens to me, buy that damn monkey a hat!
5. You remembered the Great Dane! You remembered the chandelier! But now you have to go back for the instruction manual?

6. Yes, a monkey in a nice suit with a solar calculator did this…twice!
7. That's odd because I asked for all the money in the world AND a rotisserie.
8. No big deal? It was hell to get that gecko out in one piece!

Lamborghini, for its 50th anniversary, has created a $4 million car that will be assembled for only three buyers who've already put down their deposits. I tried to put down my deposit, but I was too late. I did, however, manage to reserve the custom keychain that comes with the car, and they gave me 7-year financing so, you know, pretty good deal.

The definition of insanity as it relates to underwear: when you continue to wear the same old, ratty, devoid-of-any-remaining-elasticity underwear, even though every time that you do, it inevitably does its best to migrate south, causing you the public shame and humiliation of having to reach into your own pants to give yourself a self-inflicted atomic wedgie.

I know I'm not helping the worldwide diplomatic process, but I just kicked some guy's ass from Turkey in online backgammon three times in a row.

Three things I said that DID NOT get me out of jury duty yesterday:

1. "Convicted felons could be reformed if they just had more musical theater in their lives."
2. "I'm not prejudiced, but I hate Smurfs and believe that they are generally up to no good."
3. "Sure, I'll be on the jury as long as I can bring my Kindle, balloon animals and a large bag of White Castle burgers every day."

The other day I walked past a teenage boy and nearly passed out and died from the overwhelming whiff I got of his popular, pubescent body spray. Yes, he was an Axe murderer.

What is wrong with people? Seriously, why can't a consenting adult legally marry someone from another galaxy? A Centauri and a woman can't marry and start popping out little multi-galactic brats like everybody else? A Logopolitan can't fall in love with the earthling of her dreams? Oh, and for the love of God, whatever you do, don't get down with a Medusoid and have children! They may turn out to be hairy jellyfish with claws, teeth, and a leg? (OK...I can kind of get that one). I just can't understand why, having come so far, we can't allow two people of age who love each other to form a recognized and legal bond and walk hand in tentacle, or claw or gelatinous appendage, down the aisle like anybody else? Somebody help me out here.

AAA, the American Automobile Association, and the National Highway Traffic Safety Administration have said to forget putting your hands at the traditional 10 o'clock and 2 o'clock on the steering wheel (cue Driver Ed flashback). They now saw that having them at 9 and 3 is safer and will help keep your hands from being amputated when the airbag deploys. What the hell? I'm going to stick with the knee at 6 o'clock sharp or one hand at it's 5 o'clock somewhere.

The extended warranty gods have smiled upon me. My car battery finally decided that an undercharged life was really not a life worth living and pulled its own plug. I went down to Pep Boys expecting to take in some unwanted butt crack and buy another battery, but when we checked, my warranty was still good for one more day! Hurray for fortuitous timing! While it does not make up for the dozens of times something has broken 30 seconds after the warranty clock struck twelve and turned said object into a lemon, it was a nice reversal of fortunes.

I think that among the other serious problems facing the U.S. today, like unemployment, a terrible drought in much of the country and a less than stellar education system, we need to add something: cracked windshields. I didn't realize the magnitude of this problem until I saw that on virtually every street corner, there is a group of earnest-looking youth standing by and ready to tackle this problem. They're everywhere!

When I was in school, I learned to pass notes without getting caught. Today's kids learn how to text without looking. Damn these technologically sophisticated kids!

I have a "four-in-a-line" game on my phone that I NEVER win because the phone is just too good. It bothered me until I started doing Indian leg wrestling with my phone, which I win almost every time.

Unlike *Zoolander*, I do not have a "blue steel" look. The closest I come is with my passive-aggressive constipation look.

I bought a new smartphone, which, I have to admit, I really like. It's fast and has a great screen and, honest to God, does everything but adjust my back and remind me to zip up my pants after I pee (and there's an app for that). The only thing that was making me crazy was the battery life...or lack thereof. I could start out in the morning guns a' blazing and fully charged, but by mid-morning, my little power bar indicator would start to slide backwards faster than Enron stock. It was like a Hummer's gas gauge in stop and go traffic. It was like the Italian army fifteen minutes into battle. It was my wimpy-ass battery telling me that if I wanted to do anything other than know what time it was, I was screwed. And it was killing me. I started planning my day around phone charging sessions. My supervisors were used to me storming into their offices and bellowing, "Get the hell out of my way; I need an outlet, stat!" I started spending quality time sitting in my running car in random parking lots just watching my little green bar slowly inch upwards. After twenty minutes of quality idle time, and not unlike an 80-year-old after a couple Red Bulls and a Viagra, my battery had just enough juice to get the job done but was still nothing you would want to show off in the light of day. So the other day, I broke down and bought an extended life battery. It is truly the sumo wrestler of the smartphone battery world and makes my original battery look like the skinny guy who gets sand kicked in his face at the beach. Because it's so big and thick, it came with a new back cover for the phone, so my brand-new, sleek and sexy smart phone now has the protruding rear-end of a baboon in heat. The good news is that my phone lasts all day on a single charge. I have become smug to the point that when I see someone with a similar phone, but with the original 98-pound, weakling battery, I make sure I hold mine in a way so they get a really good look at the junk in my truck. Then, I laugh inside. So, please call me sometime. I may actually answer now.

"I can fix this and I will not get Super Glue on my fingers! I will not get Super Glue on my fingers! I will not get Super Glue on my fingers! I will not...no...no...Nooooooooooo! @#$$!!#!!@!@!#!"

Just thought of a great slogan for an underwear company: We're honored to be in your pants!

Someone called me and asked for Integers.

"Who," I asked?

"Integers," they repeated.

"Sorry," I said, "there's no one here by that name. You must have an irrational number."

It is baptism season here in California, but because of the state's ongoing water crisis, this year's baptisms are only washing away about 70% of your sins. Hey! Thanks for conserving!

You have to learn to live in your own skin, unless you're a reptile, then you have options.

I bought some spicy olives stuffed with jalapeños that are delicious, but so spicy I can only eat a handful before my stomach goes to DEFCON 5 and nuclear war is imminent in my bowels. The problem is that they really taste great, so I came up with a solution of sorts. What I have to do is wait a few days until I don't have the full, sharp, is-it-live-or-is-it-Memorex recollection of those little fireballs in my gut, creating enough steam to run Eli Whitney's pride and joy and ensuring the revenge of Montezuma's Italian cousin for a full 24 to 48 hours. When that memory has faded and all that is left is the dull, fuzzy, Neanderthal cravings of a fat guy staggering towards the fridge in the middle of the night just looking for a little somethin' somethin' to pop in his mouth that requires zero effort, I will eat a handful again. Except now, of course, I have written this and fully relived the horror that is the stuffed olives and therefore screwed myself over for the next couple of days of partaking in the exquisite horror inside that $5 bottle. This is the pits.

A farmer with only one arm was out feeding his chickens, as he did every morning. For some reason, one of the hens was agitated and trying to peck the farmer, who kept shooing it away. The hen persisted and then began to fly into the farmer, who ran around trying to avoid it. Finally, the hen flew into the farmer with such force, they both fell backwards. After a moment, the farmer got up and dusted himself off. The hen, likewise, got up and ambled away. After a short deliberation, it was ruled no arm, no fowl.

Jobs & Working

I am fundamentally opposed to this entire concept of getting up in the morning, eating a butt-load of high fiber bran bricks and then spending eight or nine hours down at the widget factory (rinse and repeat). This work thing is really cutting into freelance inventor time (don't freak out, and keep this under your hat, but I'm working on a Chia Pet that only grows sideburns) but as the bumper sticker so eloquently states, "I owe, I owe, so off to work I go."

I was on a conference call today that lasted over an hour. Only a few minutes of the call was regarding the issues at hand, while the rest of the call was idle chit chat and awkward silence. Yeah, kind of like sex in high school.

When you think about it, crime does pay. The hours are flexible. You travel a lot. And there's the opportunity to make a lot of money if you're good at it and work hard.

2:33 AM. Note to self: It does not matter that the energy drinks are 2 for $3.00. DO NOT drink both of them while driving home from work.

I had to write up and suspend an employee today. What I said: "Your actions were a clear violation of company policy, and at this time, I am going to suspend you pending a further investigation to determine your job status." What I wanted to say: "Really? Seriously? What the hell were you thinking? You are so outta here!"

When someone finds a lost item at work and turns it in, there is a generic e-mail that goes out to all of the staff. It's always something like, "A pair of sunglasses were found in the women's restroom," or "A cell phone was left in the break room," with instructions to pick the item up in the personnel office. I think it would funny to "lose" something weird, just because I would love to see the e-mail that says, "A copy of the magazine Emu Today was found in the men's restroom," or "A spiral ham was left in the lobby," or "A boomerang was left on top of the copy machine, please come by the personnel office to describe and claim this item."

So slow at work right now. In the last hour I've stapled one paper and eaten a Tic-Tac.

Being alone at the office as an adult is a lot like being home alone as a kid. Just, you know, less running around in your underwear.

Off to do an interview for a new supervisor. I have my list of company-approved questions, but I think I'm going to mix it up and make up a few questions of my own:

1. What's the weirdest place you have ever been naked?
2. Moldova...your thoughts?
3. Mary Ann, Ginger or the lady from *I Dream of Genie?*
4. How old do you think I look?
5. Be a mime for the next ten minutes while I watch.

So, I'm cleaning up my resume, and I decided that I have too many old jobs listed. These are the ones I ended up cutting:

1. National Manager of the Save the Snail Darter Foundation
2. Somali pirate (in training)

JOBS & WORKING

3. Mannequin whisperer
4. Snuggie model
5. Bovine methane gas analyzer and tester
6. Volunteer for the Unwed Mother Organization (just helping them get their start)
7. Lobbyist for the Flat Earth Society
8. Worm farmer and herder
9. Fried Twinkie-On-A-Stick franchisee
10. West Coast Inventor (edible/inflatable hamsters and dirty word pasta)
11. Hair Club model (before photos)
12. Lead singer for the band, Marsha and the Electrical Crushed Velvet Freeway
13. Butt double for nerd in Go Daddy Super Bowl television ads.

I was going through resumes recently for a job we had open, and I was amazed at some of the e-mail names/addresses that people used when applying for a job. Sexysquirrel@... might work if we were looking for someone who looks good climbing trees; otherwise, not so much. BottleofBarcardi@... does not inspire me to hire this person or let them drive or operate heavy equipment. likeamodel@... while intriguing (did I say that?) this particular attribute is not on the list of skills required to successfully do the job. Plus, I don't want anyone spending half their day taking and sending out Instagram self-portraits. Soooooobored@... makes me drowsy just reading it. I don't need Eeyore on Quaaludes or another semi-catatonic clock watcher. Bambikiller@... while I'm not big myself on either guns or hunting, I respect the rights of others to get drunk and kill defenseless animals with high-power, laser-guided, semi-automatic guns in the name of sport.

I do draw the line, however, at those who go after fictional, animated, cartoon characters. Needless to say, none of the above got the job. I kept waiting for someone to e-mail me from shortfatmiddleagedbaldguysrock@.... That's a slam dunk.

Systems are down at work. No internet. No phones. I'm banging two rocks together to pass the time trying to create a spreadsheet. It's not working.

The A/C in my car is suddenly not working. Nothing like sweating off a few pounds while driving around for work when it's 100 degrees out. Also, in hindsight, I picked a bad day not to wear deodorant.

Jobs I have turned down this month:

1. Chef at the all-you-can-eat Monkey Brain Café (country not disclosed)
2. Restroom attendant at the maximum security men's prison in Pelican Bay, CA
3. Sigmoidoscope cleaner and adjuster
4. Safety food taster/tester for Sarah Palin for any San Francisco, CA visits
5. Pizza delivery boy (car provided: 1975 Ford Pinto)
6. Extra in the movie *Glitter II* (man in clown shoes buying hot dog)
7. Assistant to the pig truffle sniffer
8. Certified aide to the colorblind
9. Freelance writer for *Fungal Times* (your toes are forever!)
10. Birthday clown for animal parties (human balloon shapes!)
11. Test patient for the new drug, Groback, for those who are losing their back hair

Am I being too picky?

Is there any better sleep than the fully clothed, drool-inducing, I'm-just-going-to-lay-on-the-top-of-the-bed-for-five-minutes (an hour and a half later) kind? I think not.

For the past year, I have had to continually fight off the urge to randomly jump up and start dancing "The Robot." I really need to stop eating genetically engineered food.

So, I just downed a sleeping pill with an energy drink. I know that seems weird, but I just love the competition!

I had to reset my password for Kaiser (health care provider) because, apparently, some genius in a cubicle somewhere decided that the password I have been using for the past 15 years was no longer secure enough. No longer secure enough? Is someone trying to hack my Kaiser account? Hmmm...I'm guessing there is a state fair carnival worker out there who wants to check my records to glean useful information so he can kick my ass in the 'Guess your weight' game.

So, every winter my psoriasis flares up a little, and this year my doctor suggested ongoing narrow band light therapy at the doctor's office (fancy medical term for fancy tanning booth) to keep it in check. I went the first time and discovered that not only did I have to wear the protective goggles, but I was given a brown, paper bag and a black sock as well. The nurse explained that in addition to the goggles, I had to wear the paper over my head to prevent any premature aging. I told the nurse, "Look at this face. Do you really think three minutes of ultraviolet light is going to make it worse? I have beautiful children specifically because I DIDN'T make them with my face." That's when she told me what the black sock was for. I was instructed to stuff my 'family jewels' (honest to God, that's what she said) into the black sock. WTF? "Hey lady," I told her, "I don't know where this sock has been, and I'm not used to giving it up to laundry items on the first date." She assured me that the sock was new (oh great...so I have to be its first time) and sanitary (if I had a quarter...). So, I got naked. I put on the goggles. I put on the sock (not as easy as you would think, and now I'm going to have a major aversion to certain hand puppets) and then put the paper bag over my head. I felt like a really perverted Chicago Cubs fan, but I have a pretty good idea of what I might be next Halloween. TMI?

Now they are saying that chocolate will help prevent colon cancer. That's great if I can just figure out a way to get it in and keep it in. Anybody?

My head and face have been so oily lately. I think there may be some illegal fracking going on up there.

So, I may have to conduct a little scientific research. You see, I'm not sure which grows fastest: tropical Asian bamboo, the giant fern tree in the Amazon rainforest or this one hair on my right earlobe that is trying to transform itself overnight into a 2,000-pound-tested tow rope or maybe something useful for bungee jumping. Hey, guys! Going marlin fishing? Sure, I'll come, but no, I do not need a pole. Don't worry, officer. I'll tie up these criminals while you go after the getaway car. Fire! Everyone, come over by this window and stand on the right side of my head!

If anyone wants to send me a "hope that jock itch clears up soon" card, that would great as I battle through this itchy situation. There's nothing worse than a condition that makes you want to walk around with a hand in your pants or makes you want to spontaneously dry hump an old telephone pole.

They made us change our password at work. Mine is so long, it wraps behind the screen. Seriously, it's so long I might start using it as a belt.

I have these antacids that are virtually impossible to open and I have to ask, why? Why do I have to channel my inner MacGyver to pry open the tiny, vacuum-sealed pill that will keep my stomach from doing the 'Hammertime' Dance almost all night? Why, in God's name, is it so critical to keep antacid out of the hands of the general public? Is there a secret government project to create thousands of frustrated, acid reflux-capable, night zombies? Are teenagers stealing Mom's Pepcid AC for the cheap thrill and dangerous rush associated with reduced intestinal acid? I just don't get it. It's possible to buy a baggie of crack on the corner in a simple, re-sealable baggie, but to score one of my antacid pills, I have to rip through industrial grade plastic with the strength of Godzilla and the surgical precision of a circumcision snip? Why?

I will admit it. I hate smoking. I never tried a cigarette, not even once, because I just didn't see the point. I don't let people smoke around my kids, and if I see someone smoking where they shouldn't be, I'm the pain-in-the-ass guy that always says something. The ironic thing to me is that no one ever starts smoking because they like it. When that kid sneaks around back with his friends and takes that first puff, he doesn't suddenly have an epiphany and shout out, "Yes! This is what has been missing in my life! It's great! I must smoke more!" He turns green and coughs and may throw up. Why would you want to continue something that makes you feel that way the first time?

I once had a crazy employee complain to HR that I was "reading her thoughts" whenever I was around her and she thought that was unfair and mean. When she spitefully told me that she had called HR on me one morning I said, "Yes. I knew that already."

There is a rumor that 3 energy drinks were stolen out of the break-room fridge this morning. No one knows who did it, but my guess is the guy who was running around screaming, at the top of his lungs, "I'm the king of the world" at about 8:15.

How to have fun at work - Change the microwave power settings to low and then watch people FREAK OUT when their Hot Pockets aren't done in 60 seconds.

Today at work, I got out of my little cubicle and spent a lot of time walking aimlessly around the building. I just wanted to see what it was like to be a free-range employee.

I don't watch Walking Dead, and I don't have to. I work for the state.

The drive to work this morning took forever. I made it all the way to song 14 on my CD (I know…what's a CD?).

I think being a professional mime would be fun, until you have a heart attack.

WARNING: Working in retail may cause changes in behavior, such as increased aggression, lethargy, depression or sudden changes in a social network. May also cause bloodshot or glazed eyes, dilated pupils, abrupt changes in weight, feeling indifferent to important events, feeling detached from your own body, hypersensitivity to criticism, insults, hurt feelings and a need to drink energy drinks by the case.

I have a label maker at work, but I don't like to presuppose things about people.

Apparently when an immediate member of the family dies, we get three paid bereavement days off; I'm looking to adopt anyone in their late 90's.

This has been the longest day ever at work. Take a couple of days like this, lay them end-to-end and you'd have a leap year.

I've been watching the clock at work so much these past couple of hours that it did, in fact, boil.

There's so many potholes on the way to work that at this point, I wouldn't mind someone filling them up with good intentions.

A Tuesday after a three-day-weekend is like the worst Monday ever.

I want a job at the too-much-information booth. "Hello! Can I help you? By the way, as of last week's treatment, I'm 100% rash free!"

That sinking feeling when the pneumatic lift on your office chair is dying and you find yourself sinking, ever so slowly, until you are eye-to-eye with your keyboard.

I scribbled, "Please see me as soon as you get in," on a post-it note, added an illegible signature, and stuck it on the computer of a co-worker before he came into work. It was hard to keep a straight face as he walked around asking everyone, "Is this from you?" It's the little things, you know?

I applied for a job with a greeting card company. I told them I'm willing to start at the bottom, in the "Blank Inside" department.

I had to do a public underwear adjustment. It couldn't be helped. Fortunately, none of my co-workers were around, but things are now very awkward with the squirrel who hangs out in the parking lot.

Work is so dead, today that I took my name badge off my belt and tied it around my big toe.

Statistically, it's been proven that the last 30 minutes at work on a Friday are like 17 hours on any other day of the week. Look it up.

We Are Family

Someone was once looking at photo of my family and wondered aloud how someone with a mug like mine could churn out such beautiful children. Hey, I didn't make them with my face!

It takes a village to raise a child, but a couple of pretty good parents with Netflix and nearby in-laws can get by.

So I have been trying to teach the twins a little Spanish. They have friends in their school who mostly speak Spanish, so I'm trying to teach them a phrase or two a week. This week, I have been teaching them how to say, "I'm your friend," (Soy tu amiga). We were all in the van this afternoon, and I prompted the twins to see if they remembered their new sentence in Spanish. They were having a hard time remembering, so I gave them a hint. "OK," I said, "it starts with Soy..."

"Oh! I know, I know!" Gracie exclaimed! "Soy latte!"

When Gracie was little she was having a hard time putting on a pair of shoes. When I suggested she loosen up the laces a little more she said, "Daddy, please! I've been doing it this way for years!" She was four.

Me: We're leaving in ten minutes. Does anyone need to go potty?

Kids: No.

Me: OK, we're leaving in five minutes. Does anyone need to go potty?

Kids: No.

Me: Alright, let's go! Last chance...does anyone need to go potty?

Kids: Daddy, no! We said we don't have to go.

Five minutes after we leave the house, one (or more) of the kids: Daddy, we have to go potty now! We can't hold it! Daddy!

Yesterday, I was showing my daughter how to use a can opener. I know this sounds weird, but the thought struck me that this is what dads and moms are supposed to do. Teach your kids all those little things so they don't grow up and have a really awkward adult dinner party moment.

I have millions of pictures of the kids. Millions. I have more pictures of the kids than my father ever actually looked at me.

I know there will come a time when the girls will spend hours on their hair and their makeup and all that other stuff that makes it harder to get into the bathroom than it is to score a four day pass for Augusta National, but for now they don't care. Many people tell me that I must be a wonderful person to have adopted four, Russian war orphans.

So the twins now have some of their Sunday school training down pat. If I comment that something is big, they will agree but add, "Yes, but God is bigger. He's the biggest thing ever." If I say that something is nice I will get the compulsory, "Sure Daddy, but God is even nicer. He's the nicest of all!" Tonight when we were putting them to bed, I told Riley that I liked her pillow because it was so fluffy. "But not as fluffy as God," she replied earnestly. "He's the fluffiest of them all!"

I have millions of pictures of the kids. Millions. I have more pictures of the kids than my father ever actually looked at me.

Men suck at grocery shopping, and I am a part of that club. If I go to the supermarket, I spend $100 on three bags of groceries and a baguette.

A new study claims that marriage drives women to drink. I'm not sure if that's true, but I'm going to ask my girlfriend just as soon as she gets back from the liquor store.

The new cat really wants to sleep on the bed with me. I keep telling him I'm not that kind of human.

Just as I was leaving with the girls to drive to my cousin's house for Thanksgiving, Riley asked how long it would take. I told her it would about 40 or 45 minutes. She thought about that for a second and said, "Oh, so about two episodes."

You know your kids aren't little anymore when you can no longer get away with that great parenting standby, "We'll see…"

I just stepped on one of the girls' necklaces and cursed Hello Kitty like Hello Kitty has never been cursed before.

I just read a fun fact. Snails can sleep up to three years straight. It didn't say, but it must be talking about snails without any kids.

Today, I shouted at the top of my lungs, "The next person who goes poopy without flushing is not getting a popsicle!"

Phone call with your significant other when you are dating: "I just called to say I was thinking of you!" Phone call with your significant other after you are married and have kids: (kids screaming in background) "I DON'T HAVE MUCH TIME!! FOR

THE LOVE OF GOD, PICK UP A GALLON OF MILK AND THE BIGGEST BOX OF WINE YOU CAN GET!!! I'M GOING TO BE OUT 5 MINUTES AFTER THESE KIDS ARE ASLEEP!!!"

When I was young, rather than have "the talk," my grandparents gave me a book that was supposed to teach me about the birds and the bees. It featured a lot of animals, most memorably a seemingly disproportionate number of chickens. Did it teach me anything? Not really. But I will say that for a long time, I knew I wasn't responsible enough to bring a dozen eggs into the world.

The twins learned a valuable life lesson this morning: Silly Putty and cats do not mix.

Take several handfuls of Cheerios, the head of a chocolate bunny, one bite of leftover pizza, a bite of something yet-to-be-identified off the floor, many mandarin orange slices, a handful of corn, a pretzel and (quite possibly) a nibble or two of the cat's Meow Mix. Eat them all and you get THE MOST DISGUSTING BABY POOP EVER! (Please don't ask me how I know).

I love my girls, but sweet, blessed Jesus, I can't walk through this house without impaling my foot on a Lego, toy ring, or half the pieces of a princess tea set! In other related news, the shinbone clearly serves no purpose greater than as a device for finding furniture in a dark room.

I ran out of my regular, manly deodorant and had to use one that daughter left behind after a visit. It seems to be working OK, although I do have an urge to skip through a field of daisies.

It's New Year's Eve, and my daughter just said that we should find a pizza place that delivers really late, order a pizza just before midnight and when it arrives tell the driver, "Oh my god, we've been waiting on that pizza since last year!"

I have decided that it's easier to have the kids clean their rooms when the kids aren't actually in them.

When I was a kid and I wanted one of my little brothers to do something they didn't want to do, I would wrestle them to the ground and sit on their faces. I called this technique, "the fart of the deal."

Spent the better part of this four-day break trying to get the girls to clean their rooms. I'm not saying they are messy, but I'm pretty sure I could have convinced FEMA that we needed some disaster assistance. When I was a kid I didn't have a lot of stuff, so keeping my room clean was a fairly straightforward affair. The girls, however, have tons of stuff. So much stuff, it lies in layers. An amateur geologist could sort down through the accumulation and clearly identify the dirty clothes era, the lost library books era and, of course, the doll and assorted doll-part era.

When I was a kid and I wanted one of my little brothers to do something they didn't want to do, I would wrestle them to the ground and sit on their faces. I called this technique, "the fart of the deal."

My daughter asked me if I liked Swiss or Cheddar cheese better. I told her I try to stay neutral on cheese, but I think she saw the hole in my story.

The cat and I had to have the whole "curiosity" talk again. He just doesn't get it.

We have a usual gravitational pull situation in our home. While it doesn't happen all of the time, I have noticed this phenomenon tends to peak right about the time the girls come home from school. For some inexplicable reason, the minute the girls walk in the door, their jackets and backpacks are subject to a massive increase in the earth's gravitational pull and are sucked down to the floor in a random and haphazard manner. A jacket may end up in the middle of the entryway floor. A backpack in the hallway. A sweater on the kitchen floor. It's unpredictable. Perplexingly, it doesn't seem to affect anything else, just jackets and backpacks. Until I get an e-mail response back from Stephen Hawking, it looks like we are just going to have to live with it.

"I have artsy, creative children!" Translation: "I can never find a pair of scissors, tape, a glue stick, a working stapler, a hole-punch or a decent pen." Yes, I am suffering for their art!

I have been trying to teach the girls that "hate" is a very strong word that should only be used for things like mosquitoes, elevator music and Internet Explorer.

My kids will grow up with the next generation of the Internet, Nanotechnology, DNA mapping, advanced robotics and hydrogen powered cars. When I grew up, we had Hot Pockets.

We are at Picture People in the mall getting our pictures done. While we were waiting, a dad with his four kids walked by. His youngest, a two-year-old boy, was strapped into stroller but wanted his freedom. FREEDOM! I know this because he was screaming like a banshee and squirming like a miniature Houdini wrapped in chains. His little body was contorted into a nearly perfect rainbow as he tried to will himself out of that stroller. As the weary dad walked past, he looked at me and sighed.

"Good times," he murmured.

"Been there," I sympathized. Instant bond.

My kids will painstaking pick out every marshmallow bit in their magically delicious Lucky Charms, tackling the time consuming project with the precision and skill of a professional bomb diffuser, but if you ask them to sharpen a couple of pencils for their homework...

If you have kids, I guarantee that at some point you've said loudly, "And this is why we can't have nice things!"

A new study says there is positive growth taking place when a child talks back. I knew I had the world's greatest kids.

The most important thing in the world is what your child suddenly decides they have to do just as you're walking out the door.

Yesterday I took the girls to the mall. As we were leaving, I saw an older gentleman in a baseball cap walking around with a parrot on his head, so I pointed it out. Gracie let out a gasp and asked me worriedly, "Dad! Do you think he knows?"

All my kids love to read, which I think is great, though, there's a certain irony in having to say, "Hey! Get your nose out of that book and get on the computer to do your homework!"

I gave the cat an intelligence test. He misunderstood my instructions and pooped outside of the box instead.

Somehow the cat has figured out that I really don't like cats. Who let the human out of the bag?

I'm a little bit color blind so I'm not sure if I'm the black, or really dark brown sheep of the family.

Here are a dad's five favorite sayings:

1. "Go ask your mother."
2. "Go ask your mother."
3. "Go ask your mother."
4. "Go ask your mother."
5. "Mom's not here? Sure, go ahead."

Three things are inevitable; death, taxes and that a kid will start counting out loud the second you tell them that they need to wait two minutes for something they really want.

One of the kids is sick, so I'm going to take a day off work tomorrow. With four kids in school, it seems like one of them always has something. I don't know how the Walton's did it. They had a huge family but they never missed an episode.

I used Google Translate when Gracie said, "I'm full." It translated to: "I'm so over this regular food, but I can still handle a gallon of ice-cream." Wow. Technology.

Becoming a father really changed my life. Imagine never having to bend over to pick something up again. They really are little miracles. Little, low-to-the-ground, super flexible miracles.

Good evening, passengers, and welcome to the bedroom shuttle! Tonight we will be traveling from Daddy's bed back to your bed. You will be flying at an altitude of about five feet. Please keep your head on Daddy's shoulder and your arms around his neck to avoid any unnecessary turbulence. Our travel time will be approximately 10 seconds. Looking ahead to your final destination, we're showing it warm and comfortable with your stuffed animals arranged to your liking. Thanks again for joining us on this short journey. We know you have choices when it comes to snuggling and thank you for choosing Daddy in the big bed. Good night, sweet dreams and I love you.

This Is the End. The Final Random-O-Rama-Dama

If you have read this far I either have some good news or some bad news for you. If you have gotten to this point of this book and think it sucks more than a four-hundred-dollar Dyson, the end is in sight. If you found a few things to be funny and entertaining, then I have scraped the proverbial bottom of the Facebook posting barrel and added this last little bit.

Nothing really scares me. I mean, I'm not particularly afraid of any insects or animals. I don't have any weird phobias. Scary movies don't bother me. I think I'm immune to all of that because I was once a member of a homeowners' association and, if you can survive that horror, nothing else gets to you.

The Paleo diet is based on eating what cavemen ate hundreds of thousands of years ago. That's weird to me because most cavemen only lived to be 20 to 30 years old, less if they were crushed by a woolly mammoth or if they pissed off their club carrying girlfriends. The exception would be the Geico cavemen, but they had all that TV money so it's really not a fair comparison. Anyway, I don't want to go on a diet where I die at 30, because that would involve both time travel and several awkward explanations.

I see a pot, I stir it. I see muck, same thing. I see the works, I throw a wrench into it. Hear that squeaking? That's my wheel.

In baseball, as in life, I'm a sucker for the high hitter.

So I had a dream last night and in it I forgot to do something and then had to go through the time and hassle to do it to go back and do it. You would think that your own dream would cut you a little slack.

I'm not sure how, but after the weekend, I ended up with a wallet full of one dollar bills. I guess if I'm shipwrecked on a deserted island with nothing but a vending machine and a stripper, I'll be OK.

I don't want anyone to read anything into this, but my spacebar is sticking.

I never learned to do origami, but when we are down to the last roll of toilet paper, I have done some pretty impressive folding and re-folding.

Fun fact: you can't write the word Mississippi without saying it out loud and skipping rope.

I don't know anything about this TV show, but *Devious Maids* is the most God awful title I have ever heard of. (Note: Please look forward to my new television hit, *Scheming Accountants*.)

My porn name is Monkey San Marino.

I just spent the last three minutes going mano-a-mano with a resealable bag that was not cooperating. That's three minutes I'll never get back.

Of all the driving offences that bug me, tailgating is the worst whether it's on the freeway or just on some street in town. When someone is tailgating me I feel like yelling at them, "We are not two dogs at the dog park trying to get to know each other better! Get your schnozzle out of my ass!"

THIS IS THE END. THE FINAL RANDOM-O-RAMA-DAMA

Did you ever walk out of a store and go to the place you parked the LAST TIME you were at that store and then think, just for a minute, that your car has been stolen and then remember that you're actually looking where you parked the last time and then walk around, resolutely, until you finally find your friggin' car? Yeah, me neither.

I'm going to download Photoshop into the mirror in our bathroom and teach it how to airbrush.

I have a zit the size of Lake Titicaca. Pushing 60 and I'm dealing with a zit that could be mistaken for a VW bug if I parallel parked my face. Now, if I could just teach it to hold the door open for me.

I have got to clean the fish tank tomorrow. It's starting to look like aquatic public housing.

Amazon is now really into the online grocery business. Remember not to shop (online) when you're hungry.

So I just left the sprinkler on in the front lawn for like 8 hours. Some people might say that I'm forgetful. No, I would argue. I'm just subliminally trying to restore America's wetlands.

The hotel I stayed at last night in Fresno had a low-flow (water saving) showerhead. Taking a shower was like being spit on by three, parched, mean-spirited geckos.

We just do not use the word skullduggery enough in everyday conversation. I'm going to teach it to the girls in hopes it spreads like wildfire in elementary schools everywhere.

Irregardless is a word. Look it up. Yet, even though it's a word, Merriam-Webster says you shouldn't use it. That only makes me want to use it more and makes me, I guess, a word rebel. Sweet.

Personal challenge...I am going to work in a "You will rue the day!" into everyday conversations.

I have no respect for semicolons. They are confusing and bully regular commas to no end.

Somewhere a study must have been conducted that concluded most people need to be prodded about 10 times to subscribe to a magazine before they submit to the pressure. At least that's about how many of those annoying, indexed-card-sized subscription forms that seem to fall out of every, single magazine I read.

I have a friend who hates the font Comic Sans to the point that it makes him angry. Ironic.

I'm going to lock my shoelaces in a room until they can work out their differences and agree that they can be the same length coming out of my shoe.

No, I didn't roll a 300 in bowling, find a 4-leaf-clover, make a-hole-in-one or win the lottery. But I did find ALL THREE REMOTES in the remote caddie at the same time next to the TV. Luckiest day ever!

Kid behind the counter: What would you like?

Me: I'll have a number three, regular size with Diet Coke, to go.

Kid behind the counter: What size?

Me: Umm....yeah, that would be regular.

Kid behind the counter: And what would you like to drink?

THIS IS THE END. THE FINAL RANDOM-O-RAMA-DAMA

Me: Still a Diet Coke.

Kid behind the counter: Is that for here or to go?

Me: Wow. To go.

I take it back. A few people really should earn minimum wage.

Scientific fact: the more you have to go to the bathroom, the harder it is to unlock the front door.

I cooked something in the oven without preheating and it turned out just fine. Betty Crocker lied and that's hurtful.

When did we become so flavor obsessed? I went to buy some sunflower seeds and was amazed at how many different flavors there are (dill pickle?). You can now buy toothpaste that tastes like pork, or Champagne or even Cola-Cola. You can get buffalo wing soda, ice-cream that is a whacky flavor mix of bourbon and cornflakes and jelly beans that taste just like baby wipes. I have been slow to jump on the crazy flavor bandwagon, but that may change with my recent purchase of Vindaloo Hot Curry suppositories. Stay tuned!

I am addicted to similes. I regularly overuse them whenever I write, and I have to stop. I don't know how to explain it exactly, but it's like....

The other day I had to pull the word "caddywhompus" out of my vocabulary arsenal. It wasn't pretty, but it had to be done.

Please join me as we search for the elusive Roku remote. The Roku remote once numbered at least four in the regions known as the living room, dining room and the master bedroom, but the encroachment of mischievous children has reduced that number to two and they are seldom seen. Sadly, these once majestic remotes now face extinction (or yet another $14.99 to replace).

It's amazing how fast we can clean the whole house when people call from out of town to say they will be stopping by to visit. What! There's a floor under there?

I'm still not sure if there is a God, but I'm starting to spell it with a capital "G" just in case.

What's with all of the "One weird old tip/trick/method" online ads today? Hey guys, we're on to you!

Unlike millions of prepubescent girls, I do not believe Justin Bieber is a god. I guess that makes me a non-belieber.

Seriously, how long do these Mylar balloons last? One just floated by and scared the living crap out of me. It seems that we always have a couple of them floating around the house at any given time, like ghosts. I'm going back to the regular balloons that float around for the day and then die peacefully in their sleep that night.

I'm pretty sure my seat belt is trying to kill me. It's subtle but it's happening.

My top 2 pet peeves:

1: People who speed in mini-vans. I mean really, that's such an oxymoron. Now, if you want to speed I don't have a problem with that. But in a mini-van? Seriously? That's like shoplifting at the Dollar Store. A '98 Ford Windstar coming up fast in the rearview mirror does not strike fear in the hearts of anyone. Chicks are not lining up to meet the guy in the Honda Odyssey who just hit 87 MPH going down the back slide of the Grapevine coming into LA. Buy a Scion and wrap yourself around a light pole like everybody else.

2. People who talk on their cell phones in a public restroom. Actually, I don't really care where people use their cell phones. I just don't understand the sense of urgency (of going to the bathroom yes…of talking on the cell phone, no). Besides, do you ever listen to those conversations (like you have a choice)? "Huh? What? Who me? Nothing man. I'm just sitting here in the bathroom in Costco trying to decide between the Chicken Bake and the hot dog combo". It's not like someone is calling you with the winner in fourth race at Golden Gate Park.

Why is a common fungal infection called "jock itch" when it is in your crotch, and "athlete's' foot" when you get it between your toes? Also, let's face it, it's not normally athletes who succumb to this funky fungus. Shouldn't it really be called something like "Fat-guy-tighty-whitey-groin-fire?" Shouldn't athletes' foot really be termed "Black-socks-with-sandals-middle-aged-man-revenge?"

Finally broke down and bought some Lotrimin anti-fungal spray. Now I've got 99 problems but an itch ain't one…

I had a daydream after 7:00 PM. My regular dream was not amused.

If you're really, really tall, I guess every pool is a wading pool.

If something is going down with my friends, I'm going to be there! I mean, I'm not going to fight or anything. I'll just wait in the car and find a really good radio station for the getaway.

I recently had a conversation in sign language with a deaf person. The fact that I only know how to sign, "You complete me," made it awkward.

I saw a crime committed in a watchtower, so now I have to go into a Jehovah's witness protection program.

My apostrophes look down on my commas. Snobs.

I wonder if fish ever look out of their aquarium at us and think, "Man, that room is really getting dirty."

Stuff was a lot easier to read when sign shakers were just sign holders.

I was talking to myself and noticed that one of us had pretty bad breath.

If you're a lousy typist with just one arm, I guess you can only hunt.

On one hand I believe in the Chaos theory as it relates to study of the behavior of dynamical stems. On the other hand, I really, really like bananas.

When I was driving home today, I stopped at a light while this guy crossed the street with a boomerang sticking out of his back pocket. I was sure he was going to get across the crosswalk then turn around and go back, but he didn't. I always suspected those things didn't really work.

I want to have a reveal party. It will be one morning to reveal if my attempt to make an omelet turns into scrambled eggs.

When the piece of toast you drop lands butter-side down, it's just the god of statistical probability's way of messing with you.

They say that if you get nervous speaking before a group, you should picture all of them naked. I don't get nervous when public speaking, so I do the opposite.

THIS IS THE END. THE FINAL RANDOM-O-RAMA-DAMA

I have seen the gates of Hell. Actually, I drove home after they dilated my eyes so, you know...

Man, it's like pulling teeth to find a good dentist!

I don't know where all the single socks go, but I hope they're together and that they've found happiness.

I'm pretty sure that in a parallel universe, I would have wax in my belly button and lint in my ears.

I get a lot of credit card offers. Some of them say I'm pre-selected and some of them say I'm pre-approved, but I'm holding out for one that says I'm pre-ordained.

I'm not saying I'm a bad dancer, but when I dance people immediately start looking for my medical alert bracelet.

A pessimist looks at the top of the fish tank first.

If you are an adult with no children or all your kids are over 16, please don't say you are "going potty" to another adult unless you are carrying around a little plastic toilet that looks like a frog.

I think they should have big billboards on the freeway outside of prisons that say, "If you were a convicted felon, you'd already be home!"

Did you ever notice that a man will always hold a woman's purse when asked, but never in the traditional purse holding manner? It's like we either have to palm it like a basketball, tuck it under one arm, or hold it from the bottom while we carry it out in front of us like we're holding a kid with a stinky diaper.

I keep waiting for them to make "The Corn Nuts Story" into a movie.

Apparently, Head and Shoulders shampoo is now incorporating the fragrance of Old Spice. So now you can wash your hair, get rid of dandruff, smell great and be transported back to 1972 with every use.

Sometimes I want to travel back in time because I know I'd be a kick ass Neanderthal.

Scientists say that DNA from a 45,000-year-old bone of a man from Siberia shows that modern humans and Neanderthals mated. That really explains a lot about a couple of guys I knew in high school. A lot.

I'm going to boycott the next daylight savings while the rest of you poor mugs lose an hour of sleep. Not only am I not going to change the time, I'm actually going to add an hour and start living large with my own 25-hour-day. I haven't worked out all of the details, but if you would like to discuss in greater detail how you can join this let's-do-the-time-warp-again revolution, call me tomorrow around five plus one-thirty.

I'm writing a list of 500 things I would rather do than get all of my tax stuff together. I'm on number 653.

Just did an income tax estimator for this year's taxes. Looks like we'll be getting back about three million. Three million no-longer-used Greek Drachmas. Looks like my underwear is going to have to rally for another year.

I don't like the word "hors d'oeuvres." It almost sounds dirty when pronounced phonetically. Let's just call hors d'oeuvres what they really are: little frozen snacks you buy from Costco that you microwave 15 minutes before dinner.

THIS IS THE END. THE FINAL RANDOM-O-RAMA-DAMA

I'm going to make a 10-bean soup for dinner. It would have been 15 or more beans, but with the economy still recovering I had to scale back.

I've been accused of trying too hard. I've been accused of not trying at all. I think my happy medium is pretending to try.

If you love someone, set them free. If they come back, keep setting them free until they get the message.

A stalk of celery only has about 2 calories, but your body uses 10 calories to digest it. So basically, a healthy diet of celery can kill you.

Sometimes people ask you a question and the response is, "It doesn't matter." From now on when someone asks me a question about something that I have absolutely no interest in, I'm going to pull a Stephen Hawking and reply, "It anti-matters." See you at the black hole.

I'm pretty sure that the cows responsible for mild cheddar cheese are made fun of and picked last in cattle dodgeball.

So went to the doctor and my tests results are it. I tested positive for being a mild pain in the butt. So glad to have good health insurance.

My new slogan for students: "Just Say Know."

I'm looking at the length of my pants legs and wondering what inspired me to buy them. I can only hope that there is a flood and I can validate the purchase.

I pierced the plastic film 3-4 times to vent, but after 5 minutes in the microwave it was still angry with me.

For the next week or so when anyone asks me, casually, "How's it going?" I'm going to look them in the eye and say, "I'm not getting enough roughage and I'd like to talk to you about it." Conversation starter!!!

I can't afford the expensive "New Car" scented spray for my car, so I settle for the "1987 Ford Taurus" scented car freshener.

I think garlic bread and popcorn secretly like to be burnt and have an unscrupulous agreement with timers around the world.

I don't want to get overtly political, but I am against any type of jelly or fruit spread (what does that even mean?) in a plastic squeezable bottle and will vote accordingly.

Waking up to a new day is a gift—a gift that I'd like to put on layaway until about noon.

I'm inherently not very good at math. Maybe it's a right brain/left brain thing, maybe I have a neurotransmitter that needs a new battery; I really don't know. I can tell you there is one exception to this rule though: when I can't sleep, particularly knowing that I have to get up in the morning for work, I become a modern-day Archimedes with this incredible ability to calculate how much sleep I will get if I can fall asleep at a given time. If my alarm clock is set for 6:00 AM and I roll over and see that it's 2:07 in the morning, my brain can calculate not just the hours and minutes I would sleep if I could hypothetically fall asleep at that moment, but also any number of random, mathematical facts associated with that amount of time. I could tell you not only how many sheep I could count during that time, but also their first names, favorite colors and political predispositions. I can tell you how many total seconds it works out to be, what North American city has a like-numbered population, as well as how many bowling alleys that town has and where the best place to get sushi after midnight is located. I can work out the statistics of my sleep patterns from the past 30 days and tell you the statistical probability on that night fitting into the mean, as well as give the Las Vegas odds on the over-under. Eventually, I'll fall asleep. When I wake up the next morning I am, once again, the Lennie Small of the mathematical world, struggling to help his fifth grader do her math homework. Oh, and I'm really, really tired…

Why does Superman stop bullets with his chest, but duck when you throw a revolver at him?

I can remember the words of every song from the 70's and 80's but still get my sock drawer and underwear drawer mixed up.

I have been trying to convince myself that I can get by on less and less sleep. It's become my new mantra. Sometimes when I nod off at work at 3:00 in the afternoon I even dream about it.

It's not a good idea to sit butt naked on a lacquered, wooden chair for an extended period.

McDonald's is trying to turn itself into Starbucks and Taco Bell is now selling breakfast. What's next? Will I soon be able to get a really good steak at Der Wienerschnitzel?

Quiznos recently announced that it was filing for bankruptcy. There was a slight delay in the filing, as the paperwork had to be toasted.

I drank about a gallon of sparkling water at dinner. Pretty sure tonight I'm going to potty like it's 1999.

I'm eggnostic; I don't know whether I believe in eggnog or not.

A pen died in my pants pocket today. It will be remembered by my left thigh and the fingers on both my hands.

I took an online CPR and first aid class. I didn't exactly pass, so if you need CPR I can only blow lightly on your face and if you're choking I can only use one arm to perform the Heimlich Maneuver. Basically, what I'm saying is if we hang out make sure you have really good insurance.

The broccoli says, "I look like a small tree."

The mushroom says. "I look like an umbrella."

The walnut says, "I look like a brain."

The banana says, "Can we please change the subject?"

Pickled beets, I've tried to make this relationship work, but I think we've reached the end. It's not you, it's me.

I really had to man up today and use the last, little sliver of my deodorant. Nothing like scraping the crap out of your armpit with the plastic edge of the deodorant in an effort to stay daisy fresh.

It's crazy, but I can make it rain whenever I want. All I have to do is wash my car.

I killed two birds, but I had to use two stones to do it. Proverb merit badge out the window.

I put way too much onion in the salad I made for lunch today. I don't even want to talk to myself.

THIS IS THE END. THE FINAL RANDOM-O-RAMA-DAMA

Facebook is adding dating profiles for singles on their site. That's cool. I've had my eye on this hot Russian bot for a while now...

Some people like to sleep with a fan. Not me. I can't sleep with all that, "You're number one, Jon!" "You're the greatest, Jon!" The giant foam finger doesn't help either.

I bought a new leather sofa and kind of felt bad about it. Then I found out it was made from free range cows so, you know...

When I was changing the toilet paper, I dropped the new roll into the toilet. The advertising didn't lie, it really is absorbent.

Finally did my state taxes. Looks like I'm going to get $61 back. Not naming names, but somebody is upgrading to 2-ply toilet paper next month!

I haven't been feeling well, so I went to the doctor and he gave me some new meds. The good news is that they will probably make me feel better. The bad news is that any chance of operating heavy machinery is probably out the window.

I'm always a little suspicious of people who can easily convert pounds to kilos and vice-versa; I'm pretty sure they must be drug dealers.

Have you ever noticed that most men (me included) are pathologically unable to open a box or a bag of food in the proper manner? We rip them open in much the same way that a wild animal will rip through your trash in the middle of the night. We show a callous disregard for perforations or any opening instructions. We want the Cracker Jacks, but we don't want to stick our thumb in the provided and well-illustrated tab on the top of the box. No, we'll just latch onto a corner of that sucker with our teeth and rip off a chunk. Resealable lunchmeat bags, cereal boxes, potato chips bags and plastic bread bags are no match for our zombie like, herky-jerky attacks on all things packaged. Now, pass the shredded bag of Chex Mix dust, please.

I think that it's cruel to make cows ingest hot peppers and spice just so we can have Pepper Jack cheese.

The Ukrainian couple next door are arguing again. I can't understand a word they say, so I always imagine it's about potatoes.

I need to work on being happier. Maybe part-time to start.

Overheard in the security line at the airport; "I'm sure they're going to question my banana."

Don't you hate it when you are having a really interesting dream, but you wake up before it ends? Then you have to wait a year before it's on Netflix?

I got busted for inattentive driving. It's just hard to focus on driving with all of this technology. And hey, these faxes aren't going to send themselves.

I'm so tired. I literally can't keep my eyes open. I'm going to type the rest of thie witgh mhy etyss cloossdde godmigght an see ou im the m0eunkg.

I started to write a profile for a dating site, but it began to sound more and more like I was trying to unload a really crappy used car so I deleted it. Now I'm going to wait until I sell my crappy used car, and hope that a prospective buyer wants to go to the movies.

I'm thinking about getting a new car. To prepare myself for the sticker shock, I went to the movies and got a large popcorn.

THIS IS THE END. THE FINAL RANDOM-O-RAMA-DAMA

I can only afford 2 1/2 Hour Energy.

Overheard: "What are you doing this weekend?" Response, "I have a long list of good intentions."

Severodvinsk – a mostly true travel story

By Jon Waldrep

Severodvinsk is a port city in the far north of Russia. Severodvinsk, or rather what happened there, is also the reason I can no longer drink vodka and have more than a mild aversion to saunas. In fairness to Severodvinsk, I was never much of a vodka drinker before, but the events that transpired when I was there in the late 1990s made vodka a dirty word to me and an automatic trigger for my involuntary gag reflex.

I was hired for a weird job in the late 1990's. I became an international recruiter for potential truck drivers from around the globe. The idea was that people would come to the U.S. as students on a student visa, take a few college classes, and drive trucks 10 months out of the year. It turned out to be mostly illegal, but that's another story.

The best part of the job was the travel. I made my own schedule and went to any country I thought might have potential truck drivers who could get a visa. In reality, I was hiring and training agents who would help ensure a steady stream of truck drivers from places like Nepal, The Philippines, Indian and Russia. Weird, I know.

I ended up in Severodvinsk, Russia, for a week because there was a good potential agent there. When I say a good potential agent really what I mean is a guy that looked good on paper.

A lot of people look good on paper. Even communism looks good on paper but we all know that in practice, not so much.

After spending a few days in Moscow, I boarded a morning Aeroflot flight to Archangel, the nearest city to Severodvinsk with an airport. Taking an Aeroflot prop plane is like letting your drunk, legally-blind-in-one-eye, friend drive you home at night in a 1972 Pinto with a full tank of gas. As I strapped in, I had the feeling I was taking my life in my hands, probably because I was. The plane was old and rickety, filled with businessmen, old women with head scarfs and a couple guy who looked like they might be KGB, able to kill anyone except James Bond in less than 10 seconds without messing up their hair.

When we landed, and after a healthy sigh of relief, I got my bag and was met by my potential agent. My first impression wasn't great. He was short and stocky, with bad skin and dark hair. He looked like a pimp, or the second or third best salesman at a mafia controlled used car lot. He spoke passable English and said, after introductions, "Now we go in my car for to go Severodvinsk." When he said the name of our intended destination in his native Russian, it sounded rich and full, like the name of a Tolstoy novel. When I said it, it sounded like a rarely performed medical procedure or a dirty word in pig Latin. I made a mental note to not say it at all if possible.

The day was cold, overcast and gloomy as we drove from the airport through a mostly barren landscape. My potential agent was explaining to me that Severodvinsk was known for its military ship and submarine building. He said that until recently the city had been closed to all foreigners and that, in fact, I was one of the first Americans, maybe the very first, visiting the place in recent history. "You will be like celebrity," he joked, "Everyone will be want meeting you!" I joked back, "I'll be like the Elvis of Severodvinsk!" He turned his head to look at me, unsmiling. "No," he said flatly, "Elvis is dead. You are not dead. And the good name is to say Severodvinsk," correcting my pronunciation. Once again, he said the name with a kind of guttural dignity, making it sound almost noble. "Severodvinsk," I tried to imitate, but my version sounded like I was choking on a soft pretzel. I made a second mental note and saved it in my brain with the same filename as my first mental note, thus overwriting it.

We reached the city limits and drove down the main road through town. On either side of the road stood a series of big, drab, nearly identical apartment blocks. They were gray and imposing, most eight to ten stories tall, many with some sort of business on the street level. I saw a pharmacy and a small supermarket but couldn't really tell what some of the others might be. There were people on the sidewalks, bundled up against the cold and shuffling their feet in one direction or the other. The whole scene, frankly, was depressing. It looked like the sort of place that might be found on an internet article entitled, "10 of the dreariest places on Earth," with the obligatory tease line, "You won't believe number 7!" I began to regret coming to the town whose name shall not be mentioned. I was less than inspired by my potential agent and, as much as I loved going to new places, the cheerless outpost we were driving though would never be on anybody's bucket list. I was thinking that dead Elvis would fit right in. I was pretty sure that I might not.

My potential agent pulled up to my hotel and insisted on carrying my bag inside. I checked in and was handed over my key. In classic foreshadowing fashion, my potential agent asked me if I wanted to go get a drink. It wasn't even noon.

"We have good vodka. Make in Severodvinsk. Very good!" To emphasis the point he gave me a stiff thumbs up. I tried to imagine him on a giant billboard, with the lopsided half-smile and the rigidly cocked thumb. I could visualize it on the outskirts of town with the slogan, "Severodvinsk Vodka. More famous than pudgy American! More famous than dead Elvis!" I begged off on the drink and said I just wanted to unpack, take a shower and maybe even a nap. If I got hungry, I told him, the hotel had a small café. He was clearly disappointed that I was not motivated to toss back a few of Severodvinsk's finest. He said that he would pick me up at 6:00 for, "special honor dinner." For what, I asked him? "Is dinner with Vice Mayor of Severodvinsk and other people with important. I go, and some friends I have will go. Very good. Very fun." I told him that sounded great and I would be downstairs at 6:00. He left the hotel with a wave and drove off in his little Russian car. I bought a couple of piroshky and headed up to my room.

A little more than six hours later I was lugging myself up several flights of stairs for the special honor dinner. I wore a nice suit and tie and a brand-new overcoat. I was hoping to look like a moderately successful American businessman. Later that night when I caught a glimpse of myself in the mirror, I decided I looked more like a moderately successful process server, on my way to somebody's backyard wedding. As we trudged up the stairs I asked my potential agent if the building had an elevator. "Elevator!" he scoffed, as if I had made a bad joke. That was all he said on the matter, so I kept climbing the stairs. A few dozen steps later we arrived at the door of the Vice Mayor of Severodvinsk.

The apartment wasn't huge, but they had a very long table that started practically in the entryway and ended near the end of the living room, enough to fit 14 of us. The Vice Mayor welcomed me in excellent English to his home and told me it was an honor to welcome me to Severodvinsk. What did I think so far, he inquired, of his city? Having been there for less than seven hours, including a long nap, I didn't have a good answer. Should I tell him that I was impressed with the quantity of stairs? I finally mumbled something about it not being what I expected. He smiled broadly. Picking up a glass of vodka he made a toast in Russian and everyone in the room who was drinking, which was everyone but me, raised their glass and knocked back their vodka.

I was introduced to the assembled guests, including the lovely niece of the Vice Mayor, a tall, curvy woman named Marina. "Welcome," she said in English, extending her hand, "I hope you enjoy your visit." Unlike my potential agent, her Russian accent was sexy, and the words rolled out of her mouth like a purring cat. I smiled and thought, oh please let me be seated next to her! Oh please! Oh please! But when the meal began I found myself sitting between my potential agent and a giant, hulk of a man named Volvo. I'm not sure if it is spelled that way but, yes, it was pronounced just like the car. Volvo introduced himself, reaching out his giant meat hook of a hand. The handshake was firm enough to cause a couple of my knuckles to pop. "Volvo," he proclaimed. "Hello, I'm Saab," I countered. It took a full couple of seconds for him to get the meager joke, then he leaned his head back and let out a deep chested guffaw. "Good!" He said. Then he got the attention of the rest of the table and, I assumed, retold my witticism in Russian. Everyone laughed I noted, except Marina. She simply smiled and nodded a polite nod of acknowledgement. Apparently, my humble stab at humor was enough to warrant another toast. I didn't understand a word of it, except Amerikanskaya, but that was fine. Everyone raised their glasses towards me tossed back another shot of vodka. I smiled broadly. I was way better than any dead Elvis.

The meal was served, and it was excellent. Volvo realized that I didn't have any vodka and quickly remedied that situation. I pointed at the vodka and asked my potential agent, "Famous Severodvinsk vodka?" He nodded happily. "Da," he said. He lifted his glass and out came yet another toast. This time I lifted my glass with the others and drank the shot. My head exploded as that jet fuel burned its way down my throat. What horrible, horrible zombie potatoes gave their life for this rut gut, I wondered? I let loose an involuntary full body shudder. It was like getting punched in the solar plexus. I shook my head to snap out of it. "Is good?" Volvo asked me. I looked at him. I'm not sure what face I made, but he found it hilarious, and began to laugh. He clapped me on the shoulder. "Funny!" he exclaimed for the second time. I really wasn't sure that I was particularly funny at that moment, but I was reasonably sure that if forced to knock back a few more shots of Severodvinsk's finest, I would become a laugh riot. A venerable barrel of monkeys. Bite me dead Elvis, I thought. Bite me.

The rest of the meal was punctuated by a number of different toasts. I lost track, but each time I dutifully raised my glass and downed another shot of the local vodka. By the end of the meal I was cognizant of the fact that I was drunk, but still hanging on to upright and functional by a thread. That would change a little later.

My potential agent mentioned that a few of the people at the special honor dinner/drunk fest were going to go out to a club and asked if I would like to join them. "That would be a big nyet, Kemosabe," I said, focusing a great deal on my balance as the room swam around me. I felt like the inside of a lava lamp. All I really wanted to do was collapse onto my hotel room bed and dream horrible dreams about mutant potatoes. Volvo and my potential agent launched into an animated discussion for a few minutes, at the end of which my potential agent turned to me and said, "Volvo says go." Volvo, nearly as big as the car his name invoked, smiled encouragingly at me. I mimicked that I was drunk by pretending to throw back several imaginary shots of alcohol. "Da!" Volvo exclaimed with unabated zeal. "Vodka!" No, I thought fuzzily, no more vodka. Vodka bad. Famous Severodvinsk vodka really bad. My head felt like it was spinning around, a la a pubescent Linda Blair.

In the end, my weak protests and clear inebriation did nothing to sway my enthusiastic comrades. We bundled into a couple of cars and headed out to, what was promised to me, the "best more famous club in Severodvinsk." Twenty minutes later we are sitting in a not quite crowded club, complete with a small dance floor, karaoke machine and the obligatory disco ball. Six of us sat down around a table near the dance floor and within mere seconds two bottles of the local swill magically appeared on the table. Shots were poured, but I begged off the first couple of rounds. I wanted to beg off the entire rest of the evening but sat there in foggy indifference while my potential agent, Volvo and three other communists inhaled their shots. After each round they joked, laughed heartily and whacked each other on the back with the force of an alternative Heimlich maneuver. Two bottles disappeared, and two full ones appeared, within seconds. Volvo looked at my still dry shot glass. "Vodka!" he bellowed, filling my shot glass to the rim. We toasted to something in Russian and knocked back our drinks. In the nanosecond that the clear liquid rolled over the rim of my glass and touched my lips I had an epiphany of sorts; this was not going to end well.

Over at the Karaoke machine a women was killing "The Sign" by Ace of Base. Killing it with the sweet screeching of a three-wattled bellbird in heat. I didn't know if it was live or if it was Memorex, but imaginary bottles of Famous Severodvinsk vodka were bursting in my head. No one else in the club seemed phased by this acid bath of warbling. Couples, and those flying solo, gyrated to the music and shuffled across the dance floor, bobbing their heads with scant regard to the nails-on-a-chalkboard vocals that the young women was belting out. My potential agent looked at me. "She's not good!" he said. "She's not best singer," he continued. Unknowingly, he did more to cement the positive, bilateral relationship between Russia and the U.S. with that single utterance than anything else he could have said. "Oh my God," I blurted out, "She makes me want to ram an ice pick into my ear!" My potential agent cocked his head, trying to process a sentence that was clearly lost in translation. Volvo said something to my potential agent, who then said to me, "Volvo says you sing now." Who me, I thought? I wasn't sure I should even stand up without an adult diaper. Singing was out of the question. My tongue felt like a bloated, wet French baguette. I was having a hard time pronouncing consonants. My voice was becoming full on, urban-legend, Rod Stewart drank gasoline like. I was barely in control of my basic bodily functions at this point, singing was out of the question. I told my potential agent there was no way I was going to sing. I told Volvo in Russian, and I don't speak Russian, that there was no way I could sing. No singing. No. Nyet. Not gonna happen. Next thing I knew, I was singing.

Volvo had grabbed my arm and lifted me out my seat in one smooth motion. The guy was incredibly strong. He marched me up to the Karaoke machine where, mercifully, there was no longer a sign of The Sign. He grabbed the mic and said, I presumed, a few poignant words about me to the crowd and then placed the microphone into my hand. The fact that I was an American seemed to pique some interest in the people there. A handful, don't ask me how many as I was still seeing double, wandered up to the edge of the dance floor and planted themselves squarely in front of the Karaoke set-up. Volvo pointed to the Karaoke machine screen and gave me a look that said, "What's it going to be, slick?" I squinted at the screen. There were hundreds of songs. Do these people never delete anything? Some of the songs were in Russian. The fact that I actually considered one was clear evidence of my sloshed state. I scrolled down the list. This was the part of the story that someone from the audience was supposed to shout out, "Free Bird!" But, that didn't happen. Finally, I saw "I Should Have Known Better," by the Beatles. That song title seemed incredibly appropriate. I pointed to it, and Volvo pushed something and adjusted something else and the next thing I knew, I was belting out;

I should have known better with a girl like you,

That I would love everything that you do; and I do,

Hey, hey, hey, and I do.

Saying that the crowd went wild would be a lie, but not much of one. There were many shouts of encouragement. I suspect that hearing someone who spoke English singing a song in English was quite the novelty in the best, more famous club in Severodvinsk. Despite my drunken state, I was rallying as I belted out the song, even hitting the high notes with some success. The dance floor filled up. Some of the patrons started to sing along, repeating the bits they knew or just making it up as they went. Even the I Saw the Sign woman was screeching in one-part harmony. There was a definite vibe in the place. Everyone in the club, except my motley crew, were either up dancing or standing in front of the small stage. As I sang it dawned on me. I was a hit. I was a big, big hit. I was the lone American in the middle of Russia's frozen north and I was a hit. No, not because I was good, but because I was a novelty. Sure, I looked more like Lenin than Lennon, but these vodka fueled dancers didn't care. I could have sung, 'Up Against the Wall Redneck Mother' wearing red, white and blue Spandex bike shorts and the crowd still would have gone wild. I had another epiphany, 2.0, wash over me like a thunderous tsunami of Russian moonshine. In Severodvinsk, at least in Severodvinsk, at least in this moment in Severodvinsk, I kicked ass. Unlike dead Elvis, I would be there all week. Sucker! Please tip your waitress.

I finished the song and got a wild round of applause, led by Volvo and his giant, thunderous hands coming together to make the earth shake. I was taken aback by my newly found fame but loving every minute of it. Volvo rolled his index finger in a circular motion, giving me the international sign to continue my evening of song and debauchery. I launched into another song, then another. I got several thumbs up from the crowd and, apparently, the I Saw the Sign woman had become my biggest fan. She hooted and hollered at the end of each song, imploring the small crowd to clap and cheer. I was just getting ready to bob and weave my way back to the table when I saw Volvo holding up his finger, requesting just one more song. Fine, I thought. I will give these fine people, my newly registered fans, an encore before I called it a night. Volvo came up again and helped me scroll through the song selections. I had done the Beatles and The Who, so I passed on any more of their songs. I had just finished a particularly rousing version of the Cure's 'Friday I'm In Love' so I wanted to try something everyone would know. Squinting hard at the screen to try and bring it into focus, I saw the perfect song to cap off the evening. I pointed to it, and Volvo nodded in approval. "Da," he said. I look over at the table where my potential agent sat with a handful of others. I didn't need to see the empty bottles on the table to realize the sorry state they were in. My potential agent had a faint smile as looked in my direction, his head slowly bobbing, dangling like a kite at the end of a long string in a light breeze. His mates were in no better shape. I pointed to my potential agent just as Volvo was starting the next song. I shouted, "This one's for you, brother!" just as the music started. I started singing.

The warden threw a party in the county jail

The prison band was there and they began to wail

The band was jumpin' and the joint began to swing

You should've heard them knocked-out jailbirds sing

And we rocked. Led by the I Saw the Sign woman, everyone in place moved to the danced floor and convulsed in unison, like they were all having a collective Pokémon seizure. I'm sure the vodka had nothing to do with it, but I have to say that on that night, at least on that night, I did more than a passable Elvis. It wasn't nuanced, but it was loud as hell and maybe the volume made up for the quality. I may have tried to swivel my hips, but it was more a function of remaining upright then trying to be sexy. I recall thinking that there was a strong chance I was going to rip my snug, suit pants right along the seam. That might have been the ultimate Elvis tribute. Volvo gave me several enthusiastic thumbs-up, looking like a cross between the ultra-hip Fonzie and the Incredible Hulk. My potential agent, and most of the others at our table, were approaching a near vegetable state. That vegetable being potatoes. They propped themselves up in various positions around the table, most with a shot glass in one hand, cigarettes dangling precariously from their lips.

I ended Jail House Rock with a flourish by swinging the microphone around a couple of times as the song was ending. As I walked off that tiny stage, many of patrons gave me nobs of encouragement. A few even clapped. The I Saw the Sign woman came up to me, took both my hands in hers, and proceeded to tell me something I'm sure was very heartfelt but, of course, in Russian. While I had no idea what she was saying, I knew that we had become kindred spirits of the Severodvinsk karaoke scene. That had to be a select group.

I got back to the table and plopped myself down in a chair. The adrenaline rush that I may have had while butchering the classics quickly dissipated. I looked at my potential agent, now looking more like a Russian statue than a Russian person, and thought to myself, "Right there with you, buddy. Right there with you." I had moved way past being horribly drunk to actually feeling horribly ill. Volvo was so happy that I just wanted to slap him. I made the motion to go and he just kept smiling. I tugged at his shirt and pointed to the exit, but he just continued to grin. Then he did the unthinkable. He looked over at the bar and stuck his giant index finger into the air. Please, oh please, I thought for a split second, let this be the big man making the international, "We're number one!" sign and not the unthinkable alternative. But we were not number one, as was made clear when yet another bottle of commie rocket fuel was delivered to our table. Volvo poured out two shots. Happily, I might add. "Drink!" he bellowed, whacking me on the back in a friendly death punch. The very sight of the vodka made me dry heave. "You're a whore bastard and I hate you." I told him. He laughed again. "Drink!" he insisted. I countered, "I hate you so much. I hate you more than ninth grade Calculus. I hate you more than some guy that the Hatfield's and McCoy's both mutually hated." Volvo just smiled, having the time of his life apparently. I was miserable, my head pounding, my stomach doing the funky chicken and my nausea level rising to a solid 9 out of 10. Volvo slid the glass into my hand. "Good!" he said, and I drank it. Then I had one more and, I think, another. I looked up at the Karaoke stage, The I Saw the Sign woman was up there, two of her actually in my blurry, double vision, killing me softly with "I Believe I Can Fly." That was the last thing I remember until I woke up the next morning.

I opened my eyes to a squinting half-slit. The bright light filling the room hit me like nuclear fallout, a million tiny firecrackers painfully exploding inside my eyeballs as the room spun slowly around me. I didn't know where I was. I didn't remember anything after blacking out in the club. I was curled up on a sofa somewhere, in someone's home, in some country, in some universe. I didn't remember anything. I could have been anywhere, but the truth of the matter was where I happened to be was of little importance. My body hurt in every conceivable way. My head was in a vice clamp and with every tightening twist of the handle it felt like it might explode. It was throbbing painfully, contracting then expanding with a steady, searing pain, churning like the viscous, hot liquid in a lava lamp. My mouth was dry as sand and my tongue felt swollen and sore and I was thirsty. So thirsty. Even the fading, floral pattern of the sofa was making me queasy. But I was more than just nauseous, one gaggy wave after another rising up to the top of my throat. I was 180 degrees past being simply hung over. I had, although I didn't fully realize it at the time, acute, ass-kicking, just-shoot-me-now, alcohol poisoning. Famous Severodvinsk vodka had beat me up and left me to die, kicking me repeatedly when I was down. I cursed the name of that swill and thought brutally evil thoughts about potatoes in general. Somewhere in my foggy brain I hatched a plan to burn down the imaginary billboard featuring my potential agent and that devil sap passing itself off as drinkable alcohol. As these thoughts wormed their way, like slow moving maggots, through my foggy brain I realized that I honestly couldn't recall a time that I had ever felt worse. This, I remember thinking, was what it must feel like to be dying. I am, I thought, at death's door. Take that potential agent! I was going to be dead just like Elvis and your objections to my quip will mean squat. Ha!

I willed my body to sit up, and that nearly made me pass out. I finally managed to shift into a semi upright position, feeling as if at any moment I might slide off sofa like an object in a Salvador Dalí painting. I realized that I was still wearing my suit, tie and overcoat, but they were horribly rumpled and had most definitely lost that new car smell. I now had a stench that screamed I had just spent three days in a back alley. I felt like crap. I looked like crap and I stunk like a mofo. I didn't need a magic 8-ball to see how the rest of the day was likely to turn out. I looked around the plain room, which continued to spin slowly around me. Thinking clearly was nearly impossible.

A women glided into the room like a blurry ghost. I had no idea who she was. I squinted hard, trying to bring her into focus. She sat down on the sofa next to me, smiling slyly. It was a knowing smile. A post hijinks and shenanigans smile. A smile that suggested that a body had been buried and I, indeed, had held the shovel. She slowly wagged her index finger at me and in a heavy Russian accent said, "You are the bad, bad boy!" Was I a bad, bad boy? What had I done, I wondered? I tried to speak, but my mouth and throat were so dry I could only croak. I swallowed hard and managed a horse whisper. "Who are you?" I asked. She didn't say her name, but simply smiled and slide a foot closer to me on the sofa.

"I always dream of live in American," she said to me, "with good American man." She smiled demurely and then batted her eyes in the least subtle manner I had ever seen. I was so confused. What the hell was going here I thought? Who was this woman? Despite my horrible physical and mental shape, I appreciated the extraordinarily surreal situation I found myself in. The last 15 minutes of my life flashed before my eyes and I re-ran them in a slow-motion recap; I woke up unsure of where I was, an utter and complete physical wreck, and was now on the receiving end of a conversation with a woman I had never met who, apparently, wanted me to become her mail order groom.

I had many questions, but before I rasp them out Volvo bound through the front door, smiling broadly. He said something to the woman on the sofa in Russian which prompted her to say, "Oh yes, I introduce myself. I am Alina. I am wife of Volvo. Volvo ask how are you." I wanted to tell her to explain to Volvo that just two minutes before he came home she was asking to come back to American with me, but I didn't. Volvo looked at me, still smiling, now shaking his head in amusement. He said something to his wife, and she turned to me and said, "I don't know how say. Like, what is this the cat pulled into the flat!" I cleared my throat. "Look what the cat dragged in," I said. "The saying is, look what the cat dragged in." Alina translated to Volvo, who found it to be the funniest thing he had ever heard. He was practically doubled over with laughter. It almost (almost) made me laugh, which almost made me throw up. Was it really less than 12 hours ago that he and I were sitting next to each other, fully sober, at the special honor dinner?

"Volvo," I asked him, "how did I get here?" Volvo looked at his wife, who translated my question. He looked at her and launched into an animated, seemingly blow-by-blow account of how things had gone down the evening before. For his wife's sake, and perhaps amusement, I could tell he was sparing no details. While he rambled on in Russia, I followed along, as if I were on the receiving end of a really challenging game of charades. Volvo, in animated Russian with the accompanying hand gestures, took us from the special honor dinner, to the best more famous club in Severodvinsk, to my stint on the Karaoke stage to what appeared to be me passing out. He looked at me and laughed and then pantomimed picking me up and lugging me upstairs in a fireman's lift.

I opened my mouth to speak but croaked instead and started to cough. I was suddenly overwhelmed by an incredible thirst. I knew I was dehydrated, and now I was desperate for a drink. I made a drinking motion to Alina. She raised her eyebrows. "Vodka?" she asked. I shuddered. Was she kidding? She was not. These Russians were trying to kill me. It was the cold war all over again.

I was desperate for something cold and carbonated. "Coke?" I whispered? "Coca-Cola?" She shook her head. She said something to Volvo and he motioned me to follow. Standing up felt like the hardest thing I had ever done. I managed to stay upright, maintaining my balance like a wobbly top. We walked out the door of their apartment and started walking downstairs. More accurately, Volvo walked and I wobbled unsteadily behind him, clutching the rail as I lurched down the stairs like Frankenstein. A half a dozen flights later we emerged out on the street. The cold air felt good. The bright sunshine did not. I squinted my eyes to nearly shut and grabbed the sleeve of Volvo's jacket, letting him guide-dog me across the street. We walked half a block, which felt like half a marathon, as I focused very hard on not vomiting. I felt my insides rise and fall like the third Reich. Volvo turned us into the doorway of a tiny, corner market and the relative dimness of the place allowed me to open my eyes. The entire place was no bigger than a moderately sized living room, with a mish-mash of products on shelves. There were a couple of old women in the place, having a rousing conversation about a can of vegetables. In my current state their voices were much too loud and really irritating. I didn't understand the words, but the sound in my head was like a novice DJ's rough scratching.

There was a wooden counter that ran across the length of the place in the back half of the store. Behind it stood an unsmiling man, with crossed arms. In my mind I named him, "Unsmiling Joe," like a character out of bad cowboy movie. I imagined he might be thinking, "What is this the cat pulled into my establishment?" I leaned forward and took the four steps that put us eye-to-eye, only the counter between us. I smiled, or at least tried to. "Coca-Cola?" I asked faintly. He shook his head. Oh, come on! I didn't want to buy the world a Coke. I didn't want sing in perfect harmony (and had already proven that beyond a shadow of a doubt). At that moment, I didn't give a rat about polar bears. Things might go better with Coca-Cola, but there was no frigging Coca-Cola for things to go better with. I just wanted to crack open that tab and chug back that sweet, fizzy cola of the gods. I wanted to feel those bubbles hit the back of my throat. I wanted to feel that unhealthy but beautiful liquid make its gurgling way down my throat. For the love of god and all that was holy, I would have given a testicle for a cold can of coke in that moment.

Unsmiling Joe stared me down. After a moment he said something in Russian, of which I didn't understand a single thing save for one word. One glorious word. The sentence went something like this; Blah blah blah blah blah blah **FANTA** blah blah blah. I looked him in the eye. "Fanta?" I asked. He gave me a curt nod. From under the counter, there were no beverage coolers in the tiny store, he pulled out two cans of soda. A can of orange Fanta and a can of lemon Fanta. I was saved! "How much?" I asked unsmiling Joe. Then I turned to Volvo and asked the same thing. I don't know why. Volvo didn't speak English, either. I pulled out my wallet and dug around. I had some rubles, but mostly I had dollars. I handed over two dollars. "OK?" I asked. Unsmiling Joe gave me a second nod. I threw the money on the counter, grabbed the can of orange Fanta, popped the tab and chugged down the entire, glorious can of Heaven sent carbonated beverage in seven seconds. A soda had never tasted so good, but I needed more. I fished out another two dollars and tossed on the counter. I grabbed the lemon Fanta, and a few seconds later it was gone.

In less than 10 minutes I drank eight cans of Fanta, four each of orange and lemon. The cans were lined up on the counter like empty shot glasses at a bachelor party. Volvo gave me a thumbs up, in the form of a question, also nodding his head as if to say, "Did that do the trick? Are you feeling better?" The truth was it did make me feel a little better. Nothing like nearly 100 ounces of soda, and the bucketful of sugar that comes with it, to help get over the massive dehydration after a night of debauchery. Although my insides were beginning to feel like a volcano at a middle-school science fair.

The two old, canned vegetable skirmishing women had been joined by three more old women, and they all now stood off to the side of counter watching the spectacle. When one looked at Volvo, he simply shrugged his shoulders and said, "Amerikanskaya." While I couldn't understand exactly what the old women said after that, it was certainly along the lines of, "Oh well, there you go. He's American. That explains everything." They continued on in animated chatter, not a single one of them wanting to make eye contact when I looked over in that direction.

We said goodbye to unsmiling Joe and the gang of five and walked back to Volvo's flat. I found the stairs nearly impossible to navigate, my head still hurting, my legs wobbly and my stomach full of carbonated fizz, looking desperately for an exit. Just as we reached Volvo's front door, I let loose with an epic belch that rolled up from my stomach and out of my mouth, a monster wave of sound and odors that forced me to relive the details of the past twelve hours. It was borscht, with a hint of pirozhki, with some massive vodka overtones and, of course, the orange and lemon Fanta. There was also another, horrible, smell. It was like death warmed over with human misery and some industrial grade sulfur. My belch went on and on, making the back of my throat click like a noisy Geiger counter. Volvo waved his hand quickly in front of his face and then held his nose. Yes, Volvo, I thought. I know it stinks. But you're lucky it made the journey via the northern express, and not the great southern byway.

We went back into the house, where Alina sat smoking at the kitchen table. She looked up from her magazine and asked me, "You are better?" I held out my right, index finger and thumb about a quarter of an inch apart. She nodded humorlessly. "Yes, I see. Last night you look the shit. Now, not so much the shit. Better." That actually made me smile. Just a little.

I asked if I could use their bathroom, and Volvo pointed the way. While I was peeing out the equivalent of the Baltic Sea, I heard Volvo and Alina in energetic conversation. I imagined it was about me but couldn't be sure. In any case, I felt as if I had already intruded on them more than enough and would just ask Volvo to drive me back to my hotel where I could sleep for the next 24 hours. I walked out the bathroom and Volvo was smiling. I didn't know if this indicated happiness by virtue of confirming I was still able to urinate, or something else altogether. Volvo spoke to me for a moment, then turned to Alina to translate. "Volvo say," she began, "that he take you now to sauna. Is good for you." Sauna? No, I thought, I don't want to go to a Sauna. I wanted to go back to my hotel, curl up into the fetal position and sleep. I told Alina to interpret that, and throw it back to Volvo, which she did. We went around and round, with me insisting I was not up to going anywhere except a warm bed. No sauna, I told Volvo with as must energy as I could muster. No. Nyet. Not gonna happen. Forget about it.

On the way to the sauna, the giant, tosspot bastard, won't-take-no-for-an-answer Volvo kept up a steady stream of happy chit-chat in Russian, none of which I understood. I called him as many mean and profane names as I could think of, some of which, I'm pretty sure, he understood. He didn't seem to mind and, honestly, I didn't have the energy to speak in much of an angry tone so I was just sort of mumbling them, one after the other. We rode in his Lada, a little, Russian econobox of a car, away from the city center towards the outskirts of town. Even with the driver's seat slid all the way back, Volvo was just able to squeeze in tightly in the small car. I had plenty of room. I watched the depressing scenery go by. I was actually feeling a bit more human, although my head still throbbed and my stomach was beginning to growl. I might have been better if the heater had not been turned all the way up, making it hotter than hell in the car. That seemed, somehow, appropriate.

We drove away from the town center, to a more industrialized area just outside of the city limits. The stores and clusters of apartment blocks disappeared, giving way to warehouses, workshops and old factory buildings, most of them having seen better days and many of them permanently closed. A few minutes later, we arrived at what appeared to be an abandoned factory. It was decrepit and more than a little creepy looking, the kind of place you would dare someone you didn't like to go to after dark. The huge cinder block building rose up three stories and ran a full block. There was an entire bank of windows that ran the length of the building. I was surprised to see that they were all intact. Any other outside maintenance had been abandoned years before, as apparent in the cracked sidewalks, the rusty fences and the overgrowth of trees near the building. We drove around the back to a parking lot. There were a handful of cars parked near a set of double doors leading the building. I still couldn't believe this was a sauna, more like a movie set for a horror film. Maybe Volvo was going to kill me, I thought, and put me out of my alcoholic poisoning induced misery.

Volvo parked the Lada (sauna-on-wheels) and we walked through the double doors into the building. I heard men laughing somewhere further inside. It did not sound as if a murder was taking place, and that gave me hope that I was not going to be killed and dumped over the side of the nearby harbor walls. Maybe, I thought, there really was a best, more famous sauna in Severodvinsk after all. We walked down a long hallway until we reached a large, square room that was part locker room, part bar. There was a wall of ancient lockers, double-stacked, across one wall. On the opposite side of the room was a small bar, with a young, baby-faced, slender man in a sweat suit stationed behind it. He looked a little like Billy the Kid. There was an odd assortment of small tables and chairs in the room, where seven men of different ages and varying degrees of attire were seated. Four of them had only white towels wrapped around their waists, one was in sweats and one wore shorts and a t-shirt. One older, heavy-set man, was completely naked. I was trying hard not to mentally judge him, bearing in mind that me naked was not exactly a visual treat. But it was tricky not to notice that he was sitting on a slatted, aluminum lawn chair that allowed his little Boris and the Russian meatballs of delight to descend down through the slates and, simply, hang there. I tried not to stare, but it was like a surreal painting, with the choice of the lawn chair causing an altered, Russian interpretation of reality.

The seven men were all engaged in loose conversation. They also each had a tall glass of beer in front of them, and young Billy retrieved empty glasses and ferried refills without being asked. The thought of drinking a beer made my gag reflex go from power saver mode to high. Some of the men greeted Volvo as we walked in. Volvo then put his arm around my shoulder and gave them, I surmised, the Reader's Digest, abridged version of the trials and travails of my recent past. They laughed, including nude guy, which prompted some seismic swaying of his thunder down under. I looked away.

SEVERODVINSK – A MOSTLY TRUE TRAVEL STORY

Volvo walked me over to a locker and started to strip. He made a motion indicating that I should do the same. I was still wearing my overcoat and suit from the day before, so I peeled everything off and stuffed it all in a locker. Volvo was down to his underwear. He looked like the real-life version of Stretch Armstrong, that large, gel-filled action figure that came out in the mid-1970s. I got down to my tighty-whities, looking nothing like an action figure, unless "pudgy, middle-aged, hung over, bald guy" counted. Young Billy brought us each a large white towel, and Volvo lost the underwear and wrapped the towel around his waist. I followed suit, less than motivated to be there, but wanting to get it over with. I had a bed at the hotel calling my name, and a toilet calling my dry heaves.

We walked down a corridor to the entrance of one of the three saunas in operation. Volvo took off his towel and hung it on a hook by the sauna door. I tossed mine up there and reached for the door handle, but Volvo put his hand on the door before I could open it. "Russian Sauna," he said smiling. "Good". He then mentally searched for the next word he said, "Hot." Volvo had been holding out on me. His English was obviously impeccable. I wasn't sure why he felt the need to state the obvious. Yes, it was a Russian sauna. Yes, it was going to be hot. Thanks Sherlock, I thought, for solving that mystery. In hindsight, I realized that Volvo was just trying to ready me for what was about to happen.

We walked into the sauna. It was the size of a small bedroom. Inside it was what I expected. Light colored wooden walls, a long, built-in bench and a heater, with copious amounts of steam coming off the rocks, stuck back in the corner. We walked into the sauna, but it wasn't a sauna at all. It was a furnace. It was a skin melting, easy bake human oven. It was a giant kiln and I was a freshly formed ceramic mug. It was

Severodvinsk's version of hell in a box. The searing heat was so unexpected that I found myself unable to breath, having been caught mid-breath as I entered. Within seconds, I began to sweat profusely, water pouring out of me and off me as if someone was hosing me down. After a minute, my eyes began to sting and burn and I had to close them. After two minutes, I thought I could smell the hair on my arm burning. I was a human pop tart.

I couldn't take anymore and bolted out of the sauna. Volvo followed behind me. I took a deep breath, filling my lungs with cool air. Volvo chuckled because, hey, what's not funny about a toasted American? He seemed completely unaffected by the sauna. I was still sweating like crazy, but my skin was slowly dialing back from lobster red to the color of the center of a medium rare steak. I wrapped the towel around my waist, made the motion of driving a car and asked, hopefully, "Hotel?" Volvo tilted his head back and roared with laughter. "Hotel?" he mimicked, "Hotel?" He continued laughing. Laughter, they say, like cold sores, is highly contagious. I actually stated to laugh as well. Hotel, I asked myself, what was I thinking? Hardy, har-har.

Wearing only our towels, we walked back to the bar where young Billy automatically set two tall glasses of beer in front of us. What was it about this country and the nearly instantaneous service when it came to alcohol? Volvo lifted his, clinked it against mine, and drank the whole thing in three, big gulps. The idea of putting more alcohol into my body was awful. Then I thought, what the hell? Hair of the dog, right? Burning hair of the dog. Better to drink this so we could be on our way. I downed the beer. It was better than I expected and the cold liquid tasted good and replenished, at least a part, of the body fluid I had just lost. I set the empty glass down on counter. Young Billy moved to get us another beer. Although the nearly non-stop pounding in my head had settled into a dull thump, thump, thump and the queasy feeling in my gut was a bit better, I didn't want to push my luck. I gave young Billy a moderate death stare and a running stream of 'nyets' and he stopped in his tracks. That made Volvo laugh again. I was glad that I was able to provide such a steady stream of entertainment to my hulking, Russian friend.

Another man walked into the room. Volvo stood up as and greeted the man as if he had been expecting him. The man walked over to us and shook Volvo's hand. He looked to be in his early 60's, with a military haircut and a ramrod straight stance. He also had an unsmiling, weasel face. He wore a very nice sweat suit, adorned with several patches, some of them depicting sports but most of them with the word, Russia, along with some type of logo. He and Volvo spoke of a few moments, and the man's expression never changed once. Volvo introduced us, searching in his mind for a word in very limited English to call the man, before settling on, "Coach." Coach Weasel Face and I shook hands, his grip was vice like and I was sure that he could break every bone in my hand in he wanted to. He looked me in the eye and asked, "Amerikanets?" Are you American? I nodded my head in affirmation. For the first time, I thought I detected the slightest smile from Coach Weasel Face.

Volvo walked in the direction of the sauna, not the lockers, and I found myself not believing that we were going back into Dante's inferno. We got to the door of the sauna and Volvo put up a finger, indicating that I should wait. Coach Weasel Face walked out somewhere, returning a minute later with a large, mental bucket filled with liquid and a couple of short tree branches, each about three or four feet long, with one half in the liquid and the other half sticking out of the bucket. The liquid looked like oily water and smelled strongly of something like eucalyptus. I assumed that the water was to pour on the rocks in the sauna's heater. I was wrong.

Coach Weasel Face stripped down efficiently and quickly, folding his sweat suit and leaving it on a nearby chair. He had on a pair of gym shorts, which he didn't take off. Volvo threw his towel back on the peg and walked into the sauna. I let my towel drop to the floor, but Coach Weasel Face gave me the stank-eye so I hung it up as well. I walked back into sauna with Coach Weasel Face, carrying his bucket, right behind me.

Knowing what to expect made it a little, a very little bit better. I was still overwhelmed by the heat, but I was not shocked as I had been the first time. I had taken a deep breath before going in, having learned that lesson. I had about five seconds to think these thoughts when Coach Weasel Face pulled one of the branches out of the bucket and swatted me hard on my lower back and butt. The branches made a loud 'whap' sound as they hit my skin. I jumped up and started to say, "What the hell!" when he smacked me again, even harder. I noticed that he had drawn blood, and it mixed together with my sweat and trickled down my leg into the drain in the middle of the floor. I was pissed off and turned towards Coach Weasel Face to protest. That, as it turned out, was a bad decision. Just I was turning he was bearing down on my again. I just enough time to cover up my privates before the branch hit me on the side and top of my thighs, catching my right hand full on. This time he loudly shouted out, "Amerikanets!" as he swung the branch. Great. I was going to pay the price of the cold war in this sauna. Naked. Roasting. Bleeding from have a dozen nicks on my body. Still feeling the effects of the night before.

SEVERODVINSK – A MOSTLY TRUE TRAVEL STORY

Coach Weasel Face got in one more shot, on my back, before I bolted from the sauna. I closed the door behind me and, once again, sucked in some cool air. I heard the sound of more branch whacking inside the sauna. I assumed that Coach Weasel Face was now going after Volvo. Either that or having accomplished his life goal of torturing an American, he was whacking himself to a glorious death, taking one for the Ruskis. That proved to be false when, a couple of minutes later, Volvo, ever smiling, the bastard, walked out with Coach Weasel Face in lock step behind him. Volvo, sticking to the routine, gave me yet another healthy smack on the back and then laughed. I was turning into a regular court jester, apparently. Coach Weasel Face scowled at me, but I did my best to maintain eye contact despite the fact that he scared me shitless.

Volvo grabbed his towel and I did the same. Coach Weasel Face just left his gym shorts on. We walked back to the locker room-slash-bar and sat at a table. Young Billy had three beers set down in front of us before I had time to protest. To be honest, I was too stunned and overwhelmed to do much more than sit there. I could feel the sting on my back and on my ass from the branch beat down I had just endured. I looked at Coach Weasel Face. He stared back at me with his flinty eyes.

"You're kind of an asshole," I told him.

He smiled and replied, "I have been called worse."

Great. Coach Weasel Face had been holding out on me. Wow. Just wow.

"Why didn't you tell me you spoke English? I could have been calling you all kinds of stuff."

"You didn't ask me," he said. His English was excellent. Son of a monkey.

Volvo downed his beer. Coach Weasel Face explained that the (literal) bush whacking he had given me was the perfect remedy for a bad hangover. The combination of heavy sweating and being swatted was, he said, the textbook combination to get over an excess of bad vodka and karaoke singing. Volvo, apparently, had not be discerning. Coach Weasel Face told me that he had coached Volvo as a wrestler and boxer, before Volvo had moved on to kick boxing.

Looking at Volvo, he said, "He's very big and strong. He could have been a very good boxer, but he likes the night life and the drinking just a bit too much. He's a good man, but sometimes a bad boy."

I pondered that, but not very hard. I also, what the hell, drank my beer. Inexplicably, I let Volvo and Coach Weasel Face talk me into going back into the sauna. I just didn't have the energy to protest and I suspected it wouldn't have mattered. In and out we went, three more times. Each time Coach Weasel Face swatting me with the branches, each time feeling like a dozen sharp clawed, crazed cats trying desperately to climb up my backside. I suppressed some yelps of pain, while others escaped. I said some very bad things about mother Russia. Coach Weasel Face just snorted at each of these, coming as close as I imagined he could come to actually laughing. After each session in the sauna, we went out to the beers young Billy had ready. Back and forth until finally, as I staggered out of the sauna for the fifth time, Coach Weasel Face said, "We're done. You lived. Something to tell the kids about, eh?" Maybe, I thought. Although if I hadn't covered up my baby making region while I was being pummeled in the sauna, the option for any additional children might have been off the table.

SEVERODVINSK – A MOSTLY TRUE TRAVEL STORY

Coach Weasel Face put on his fancy sweat suit, shook hands with Volvo, and left. Volvo led me to a room with half a dozen showers, and I took a long shower in tepid water. There was bar of, honest to god, industrial strength soap-on-a-rope hanging off the shower head and I used it liberally to soap up and rinse off. Rinse and repeat. Rinse and repeat.

Volvo was already in the locker room getting dressed when I walked in. I started to do the same. Young Billy, behind the bar, lifted an empty beer glass and nodded expectedly, asking me without words if I wanted one for the road. I shook my head no but grabbed a twenty-dollar bill out of my wallet and walked over to place it on the bar counter. "Spasibo," I said to young Billy. Thank you in Russian. He seemed please.

Once dressed, Volvo and I walked back out to the car. The skies had cleared and the sun was trying to peek through them. The air was still cool, and it felt good to be outside. I realized that my head was clear and no longer pounding, and the only signal my stomach was sending me was its need for sustenance. I had renewed energy and felt, remarkably, great. It was crazy. Volvo looked over at me and asked, "OK?" trying to gauge my general state of well-being. I looked back and said, with complete honestly, "Volvo, all kidding aside, I have never felt better," and for good measure I whacked him on the back for a change. Since I knew he didn't understand a word I had just said I gave him a thumbs-up as well. He nodded in approval. I made an eating motion, and Volvo nodded in agreement. We were both starving.

We climbed into the Lada and drove back into Severodvinsk.

Dead Elvis had left the building.

THE END

Barbara Ham from Canada

A short story by Jon Waldrep

The shoe didn't fit, so she couldn't wear it.

I smiled what I hoped was my most cheerful, retail smile and added another shoebox to the ever-growing reject pile. The woman sitting in front of me was a regular at Ken's Shoes, showing up every few weeks in hopes that our latest shipment would contain a miracle, something stylish yet comfortable in a women's size 10, extra wide. She was a large woman, in her early forties I guessed, with light brown hair that was beginning to gray. One of the other salesmen had once called her Drizella, after one of Cinderella's glass-slipper-challenged, mean-spirited stepsisters. While that was totally not cool, the name had stuck despite the fact that she was actually very nice and cheerful, and it was hard not to admire her unfailing optimism in finding a nice pair of shoes that fit.

I was often given the challenging customers, like the ones with particularly large feet, or the ones not likely to buy anything after looking for hours, or the families with a half-dozen, rambunctious, sugar-fueled kids running up and down the aisles like a thunderous pack of out-of-control howler monkeys. When I was working and anyone like that walked through the door, Dave Gonzalez, a 50-ish former punk rocker and our store manager, would typically give me a subtle heads up and ask, "Why don't you help those guys out, Drew?" He knew I wouldn't mind. He said I was 'imperturbable' and that was a good quality to have when dealing with people. I told him I was going to add that to my resume under 'special skills.'

I grabbed the stack of boxes and told Drizella (Not cool. I know) that I would check in the back to see if there was anything else she could try. I already knew there was nothing else back there that would fit, except maybe a pair of men's boots, but at least it would appear that I was doing my best to follow through on the Ken's Shoes motto: "We will find your perfect fit!" Catchy, but not always possible.

I had been working part-time at Ken's Shoes for just over a year and had spent my very first month stuck in the back room, with its high shelving units and row after row of shoe boxes. For a solid month I was all about stocking and organizing, so it only took me a couple of minutes to put back the several boxes of too small shoes I had lugged out. I took one last look around for something, anything, that might fit Drizella. As always, I double-checked for any hidden pair of shoes that might have been tucked away, or overlooked, but couldn't find anything. I headed back out to the sales floor to tell her that, at least for today, we were out of luck. She smiled and thanked me for trying. More than once I had thought of suggesting that she look online, where I was sure there were dozens of sites specifically dedicated to size 10, extra-wide women's shoes, but I suspected she just liked coming into the store. Maybe because it gave her something to do, or maybe it was just for the human interaction. We had become, I imagined, part of her routine. She said she would check back in a few weeks to see if we had received anything new and I agreed that was a great idea. I also resolved to learn her name the next time she came in. At least she was always pleasant and smiling; that wasn't true of all our regulars.

For the last year I had been juggling a full load of classes at the university together with the 25-hours-a week or so Dave would pencil me in to peddle shoes, socks, laces, and polish. It was a good part-time job. Dave was laid back, and we spent a lot of time talking about books, bands and the general state of the universe. We particularly bonded over music. Dave was a music fanatic and a passionate collector of original vinyl albums. He had also played in a local punk rock band when, he said, dinosaurs roamed the earth. He had broadened my musical horizons well beyond whatever was currently on the top of the charts and introduced me to music from bands and artists from the 1960s to the 2000s to whatever was the latest and greatest that week. It was one of the best perks of working at Ken's and a day rarely passed that we didn't talk about music. When I was working and the store was empty, Dave would sometimes call to me across the sales floor from the door of his small office.

"Drew!" he would yell, "You've got to check this out!" Then he would blast something over the store's prehistoric PA system, either off his computer or using the ancient turntable that he had hooked up in his office. I never had any idea what kind of music, or even from what decade, he would play but it was an amazing musical tutelage and it made working a shift something to look forward to.

The other salesmen, with one exception, were cool. At the moment it was all guys. Our lone female salesperson had left a month earlier to become an assistant manager at one of the town's movie theaters. We held a small going away party for her when she left. I think we were all secretly hoping that she would become our connection to free movie passes and discounted popcorn.

Just as Drizella left, a man walked briskly into the store, surveyed the landscape, and then walked right up to me.

"I want," he began quickly, "a pair of tennis shoes, all white or mostly all white, size nine, for less than $50."

"Are you using them to play a sport, or to just walk around and look flashy?" I asked.

He smiled. "I got roped into coaching my daughter's rec league basketball team this summer."

I walked him over to the athletic shoe section and picked up a low-top, basketball shoe.

"These," I told him, "are durable and comfortable. Mesh and foam uppers. Solid but not too heavy, and they have gel foam insoles. They'll break in after you wear them a few of times, and should get you through at least couple of summers, no problem."

I handed one over to him. He turned it around in hands, poking at the insole.

"How much?" he asked.

"Forty-six dollars and change, out the door."

"Sold," he said. He didn't bother trying them on; he just took the box up the front where Dave rang him up.

I mentally calculated my 2.0% commission. It wasn't a lot for one pair of shoes, but it added up every two weeks. The commissions, plus the whopping $11.00 hourly wage, helped me survive the school year. Between my financial aid, the money I made from work and some occasional cash from my parents, I could afford to pay my share of the rent, split three ways between myself and two roommates in an apartment near campus. I could also buy just enough gas for my ten-year-old Honda to keep the gas light from flickering, and my text books (which in case you were interested, are crazy expensive and feel like the biggest scam in the free world). While my disposable income was limited, it allowed me to eat just about all of the PB&Js, Ramen noodles, pasta and assorted cereals I wanted, while occasionally splurging on Sushi or some Pad Thai noodles on the weekend. I also had a couple of hundred dollars in the bank that I was trying not to touch. The front brakes on my Honda were squealing in protest every time I stopped and would need replacing soon.

Between school and work, I was pretty much on auto-pilot, getting out of bed every morning and double checking my schedule before heading out the door to whatever combination of class and shoe selling I happened to have that day. Sometimes, when motivated, I even studied. I wasn't motivated very often and mostly just read for pleasure instead of for class. Somehow, I managed to pass all my classes, which was either a testament to my intelligence or a sad indicator of my coursework as an English Lit major. More the latter, I was sure. If anyone asked me what I was going to do, my standard reply was, "write the next, great American novel." Lately, I had also been working on a movie screenplay about zombies. Yeah, I know, very late to the party on that one.

After three years of college the truth was I was just putting one metaphorical foot of higher education in front of the other as I worked towards my apparent dream job of wearing the natty blue uniform of a full-time employee at the local post office. No, not really, but that's where I feared I might end up if I didn't get my shit together and decide what I wanted to be when I grew up. I was looking forward to finishing the last few weeks of classes before summer, where I could put off any major decisions for a few months.

I glanced around the store. There were no other customers for me to help at the moment. That wasn't unusual for a Friday morning. People would start coming in soon as it got closer to lunch time and we would probably stay busy for the rest of the day.

I didn't have class on Friday and, as often was the case, had basically rolled out of bed and drove to work. I had skipped breakfast, so I was getting hungry and looking forward to my lunch break. When I was working at Ken's I usually didn't bother to bring anything to eat. If I was only working a four-hour shift, I didn't need to. If I was working a full shift, I would get Mexican or Chinese from one of the restaurants near the store.

I walked the sales floor, trying to look like I had something to do. I carried away a few more boxes of shoes and took them to the back room, where I organized a row of kid's shoes that was all out of whack. As I walked out of the back room, I nearly collided with Emil, the only full-time salesmen and, in my humble estimation, a pretentious prick. He was the only person in the place I could happily live without.

"Jesus H Christ!" he huffed, taking a step back. "Watch where you're going!"

I muttered a, "sorry, my bad" as we passed each other through one of the four doorways that connected the sales floor to the back of the store. I imagined there would be a new sign in the break room, warning of the dangers of speeding blindly through these doorways. Emil, the self-appointed captain of the non-existent safety team, made a habit of posting carefully handwritten signs and notices whenever he felt any of us minions had stepped out of line. My favorite was a little ditty that read, "Your lunch break is 30 minutes long. Not 29! Not 31! Exactly 30!" Poetic.

Technically, Emil was just another salesman, but because he was full-time and had worked at Ken's Shoes even longer than Dave, Emil thought of himself as the de-facto manager. He was only a few years older than me, but he was already doing what he wanted to do for the rest of his life. That made me both sad and envious. Aside from aspiring to sell more shoes than the rest of us combined, Emil's only other goals in life were to become a store manager one day and to buy a Corvette. The Corvette, makes and models, was the one thing we could talk about with any semblance of friendliness.

It was thought that Emil had been passed over for the actual store manager position at least twice. The rest of us didn't know if that was what lead to his generally aloof behavior with the rest of us or, as it had been suggested, he was simply born with a stick up his ass. I think Dave tolerated him because Emil was the prickly enforcer of the rules---real and invented---that Dave didn't want to be. Dave was mellow, soft spoken and thoughtful. Emil, at least around his co-workers, was usually all clenched up like the guy next in line to get his prostate checked. There was a second, much more important reason that Dave put up with him. The truth was that like him or not, Emil could sell shoes like a motherfucker, or as Jorge, one of the other part-timers had once said, "Como una máquina." Literally, "Like a machine."

When a customer walked through the door, Emil would flip a switch and become the most charming, consummate salesperson I had ever seen. It was quite an amazing transformation. A customer who may have been "just looking" when they walked in the door would often leave with two or three pairs of shoes and an assortment of polishes, water repellants, and replacement laces after Emil had latched onto them. While Emil scooped up most of the good customers and sold by far the most shoes, the rest of us were content with whatever scraps were left over. Yes, he could be a jerk to me and the other workers, but in his salesman mode he could make old ladies swoon, children laugh with delight and generally charmed the pants off most of the attractive women who came into the store. Rumor had it that had actually happened on a few occasions.

I wandered around, straightening the displays, nudging the foot measuring gadgets (shoe sizers to those of us in the know) out of the aisles and under the orange and brown, Naugahyde-covered chairs that were bunched together in rows of four. Dave was paranoid about someone tripping over one and suing the store out of existence, so we all made a habit of scanning the aisles for strays whenever we had nothing else to do. I had tripped over them more than once, the last time needing to execute a full-on version of a tuck-and-roll just to keep from landing face-first onto the earth-toned carpet. When I sprang to my feet, I noticed that every customer and employee in the place at the time was looking my direction.

"Thank you," I said. "I'll be here all week. Remember to tip your waitress!" I then walked stiffly to the break room in the back to recover, mostly my self-esteem.

Customers began to trickle in, so for the next hour Emil and I, along with a recent addition to the staff named Jeff, stayed busy. Dave was in and out of his cubby hole of an office, helping when needed, but mostly just chit-chatting with the customers and running the cash register. Jeff, who I had only worked with a couple of times at that point, asked me a question about the girls' light-up princess sneakers. I couldn't tell him exactly how long they would continue to light up, but I knew we had customers who had worn them over a year and they were still flashing with every footstep. I told him to wow the 4th grader and her mother with that tidbit of knowledge.

"Thanks, Drew," he said as he walked back to them.

As we got busy Emil zeroed in on what he thought were the best customers, guessing right most of the time, and sold box after box of shoes. I sold a pair of retro canvas, high tops (very popular), some expensive hiking boots and a pair of shiny, black Mary Janes to a 5-year-old girl and her mother.

"These are going to be my church shoes," she confided to me. "If I wear them outside to play my mother will kill me."

Her mother forced a smile and threw me an exasperated expression, as if to say, "These kids!"

I gave the daughter the wink of fellow conspirator and walked them both to the front where Dave continued to ring up customers, sending them off with a polite, "Thank you for shopping at Ken's."

Dave motioned me over to the counter. "Guess what I found?" he asked. I knew he was talking about some new album that he had bought on either eBay, Craigslist, at a garage sale or in one of the few remaining good record stores in northern California. Dave had an impressive collection of vinyl and spent much of his free time perusing the internet in search of like-new, original issue, vinyl LPs. "No re-issues!" he had told me on more than one occasion. "I want to hold the same record that some kid paid three dollars for in 1970. I want to listen to it the like dozens, maybe hundreds of other people did before me. A re-issued LP is just a piece of vinyl. An original issue is a piece of history."

I knew that Dave had a couple of "Holy Grail" records on his list, but if he had found one of those, he would certainly be freaking out and playing it over the store's speaker from the turntable in his office. That had only happened once since I had been working at Ken's, when Dave found a like-new, 1979 issue of *The Fine Art of Surfacing* by the Boomtown Rats that he played non-stop one Saturday.

"Let me guess. You finally found that mint condition copy of *Combat Rock*," I said.

He laughed. "You're funny," he said. "A real laugh riot."

I had thrown out the name of a Clash album that I knew Dave was desperate to find. It was his current pursuit and I knew that it would be an incredible discovery when, and if, he could find a pristine, original copy for his collection.

"I'll have you know, I found a beautiful copy of *Diamond Dogs* at The Works yesterday," he said. The Works was a hole-in-the-wall record store downtown, where Dave was a frequent visitor. "They put it aside for me because they were sure I would buy it, and I did." Dave then launched into his habitual discourse about how digital music lacked the deep, rich sound of vinyl. There was no doubt that we would be listening to some David Bowie later.

I was surprised when I looked up to see it was nearly noon. I was scheduled to take my lunch at 12:30 (exactly 30 minutes!). As far as I could tell by looking out the front windows, the morning fog had burned off and it was just another beautiful, end-of-April day in northern California.

I had found a wadded up twenty-dollar bill in a pair of jeans a couple nights before, so I was contemplating my lunch options. Ken's Shoes was in a small strip mall with half-a-dozen other businesses, located on the edge of town. You had to pass it to get to the highway, and the university 10 miles away, so there was almost always a steady flow of one-way traffic in front of the store. Behind the mall, the road ran one-way in the opposite direction. The only thing over there was the small, Greyhound bus station and a tire shop. The shoe store had a Kinkos on one side, a beauty supply store on the other, and a little hole-in-the-wall Chinese take-out at one end of the mall. The food there was good, if you could eat it while overlooking the generally grimy interior of the place. They had managed to squeeze two tiny tables in the front of the restaurant so you could eat there if you wanted, which is exactly what I did on nice days.

If you crossed the street at the end of the mall, there was a placed called "Taco Tyme." Once it had been part of a restaurant chain called "Taco Time," but when that relationship ended, the owners had simply replaced the "i" with a "y" and called it a day. I don't know why exactly, but I found that appealing. I liked the fact that Taco Tyme, like Ken's Shoes, wasn't part of a big chain. I ate there a lot when I worked and after a year I knew that menu work-for-word. There weren't a lot of other food options nearby. If you wanted a fast-food burger place, you had to walk past the other end of the mall for about three blocks, where there was a cluster of the usual suspects on three of the four corners of the intersection.

It was while I was contemplating lunch, and the meaning of life (but let's be honest, mostly lunch) that a girl walked into Ken's. I say "girl" because I was more accustomed to saying "girl," as in "talking about girls" and, on those rare occasions when one of my roommates dragged me off to some random party, trying to "pick up girls" with a disconcertingly low success rate. What I should have said was that while contemplating lunch, a *woman* walked into the shoe store. I immediately knew two things about her. One, I found her strikingly attractive and two, she was about five feet, six inches tall. The second part was easy because of the height indicator tape we had on the inside of the doors. Supposedly, the tape was there to better gauge the height of anyone who robbed the store. I was pretty sure she wasn't going to rob us, but if she did, I would be the first guy in line when the police asked for a description.

She looked my way and smiled. She was about my age, with copper red hair, tightly curled into tiny ringlets that cascaded down past her shoulders. Even from where I stood, I could see a light dusting of freckles across her face, on her cheeks and across the bridge of her pixie nose. She was wearing a t-shirt with a picture of the Beatles Abbey Road album cover on it---the one with John, Ringo, Paul and George crossing the street one morning in August of 1969, outside EMI Studios on Abbey Road. She coupled that with an off-white skirt, a wide, leather belt and a pair of black, Van's shoes. Aside from my acquired knowledge of shoes, I knew nothing about fashion, but I had a pretty good sense of when people wore clothes that suited them, not just in size, but also personality. I liked her look. The fact that she was wearing a Beatle t-shirt only made me double down on my opinion.

I took a step in her direction but before I could say hello, Emil swooped in from out-of-nowhere and, before I knew it, was greeting her with his 1,000-megawatt smile and a cheery, "Welcome to Ken's. How are you today?"

I watched as he launched into his routine. I really, *really* hated Emil at that moment and my mind began to concoct a few, very choice signs of my own that I would like post in the break room.

Even though I couldn't hear the exact words as I turned away, I knew the drill. The expansive welcome. The charming chit-chat. The light chuckle at his own joke. The ability to size up exactly what the customer wanted, even if they customer didn't know themselves. I had to give it to him, Emil was good. Damn him. I walked back to the register and, resignedly, turned to watch him do his thing.

The performance continued for a few more seconds, but then something strange happened. The woman said something to Emil, pointed over at me, and smiled. Emil's smile froze in place, like a waxed museum movie star. He looked at me with his head cocked slightly in puzzlement and a barely discernable squint of his eyes. He looked at her, then back at me, and once again at her like he was processing a lot of data. You could almost hear the gears turning in his head. Finally, he said something to her, forced a broad smile, gave her a polite nod and briskly walked in my direction towards the back of the store.

As he passed me he hissed, "No personal visits at work! Look it up." He continued walking until he disappeared through one of the doors leading to the back room.

I looked back where the woman continued to stand patiently, looking at me. We walked towards each other until I found myself face-to-face with the person who had done something I had never managed to do myself: make Emil go away.

I reached out my hand. "Hi, I'm Drew. Nice shirt. I have some Beatles in my t-shirt arsenal as well, but not that one. It's on my list."

"Hello Drew," she said, taking my hand and shaking it firmly, "I'm Barbara Ham, from Canada. Do you always shake hands with your customers?"

I dropped my hand to my side. "Only the ones who make Emil disappear." I replied. "Do you always tell people you're from Canada?"

"I was told Americans think it's quaint. Does it make me seem charming, but just a tiny bit quirky?" she asked teasingly, holding up her right hand with her index finger and thumb just an inch apart to indicate 'a tiny bit.'

I wasn't sure how to answer. "Yes?"

"Excellent!" she exclaimed. "That's just what I was going for. I'm so glad to see it's working."

"By the way, if it's not a Canadian state secret, what did you say to him?" I asked.

She smiled, "Oh, that? I told him that I had come to see my boyfriend and that, in fact, you were said boyfriend. That you also have some t-shirts of the greatest band in the history of music is a sign that I have chosen my fake boyfriend wisely."

That caught me off guard. "You're going through an awful lot of trouble just to get my coveted twenty-percent employee discount."

She peered at me with her very green eyes. "Yes, I'm very sorry I dragged you in to this. I'm just killing some time and he seemed so..."

I cut her off. "Overbearing? Phony?"

"A bit, yes," she agreed. "I have a few hours to kill before I get back on my bus. I didn't want a shadow while I was in here, especially since I'm not going to buy anything."

"I don't think you heard me when I mentioned my twenty-percent employee discount," I said. "What kind of fake boyfriend would I be if I didn't offer it to you?"

She laughed. "All right. I'll look around and maybe, just maybe, I'll buy something. Oh, and Drew, so far you are one of the better fake boyfriends I have ever had. Top five, anyway. OK, off I go to check this amazing selection of shoes."

I couldn't think of anything clever to say. Nothing. Finally, I blurted out, "We'll find your perfect fit!" just a little too enthusiastically, and then immediately regretted it. *I'm an idiot*, I thought.

She pursed her lips and rolled her eyes slightly, bemused at my random outburst. I watched her make her way to the women's shoe section. I remembered I was still on the clock and wandered over to the cash register where Dave had just finished ringing up a customer.

"Thanks for shopping at Ken's Shoes. Come back again!" he said as customer with a new pair of loafers headed out the door.

"Busy today," Dave observed calmly.

"Yeah," I replied, trying very hard not to stare across the store at the tiny bit peculiar Barbara Ham from Canada.

Jeff walked up to the register with a family and four boxes of shoes, setting them down on the counter for Dave to ring up.

"Dude," he asked me under his breath, "is that really your girlfriend?"

How could be possibly think that? Where was getting his intel? I tossed that thought aside for the moment. If I said no, Jeff would tell Emil that he had bad information and Emil would undoubtedly swoop back in and pester poor Barbara Ham right out of the store. My fake boyfriend ranking would go in the toilet. It occurred to me that I didn't want Barbara to leave the store, and certainly not because of the boorish Emil. I looked up at Jeff and gave him a thumbs up.

"Don't tell anyone" I said.

"No problem, man. You got it," he replied, adding "She's hot, man. You're lucky."

"I know." I said. "Thanks."

Jeff wandered off to help some customers. Dave finished ringing up someone up, sliding the shoe box into one of our orange plastic bags. As that customer walked out the door Dave turned to me. "Emil says," he said, pointing a quick finger in Barbara Ham's direction, "that's your girlfriend."

When had Emil come out from the back room, let alone talk to Dave? Emil had sulked off and hadn't been anywhere near the register. I looked around. I spotted Emil on the other side of the store helping a customer. He glanced over at me, his eyes still narrowed in suspicion.

I looked over at Barbara Ham and caught her eye. She was holding a fairly hideous sandal, adorned with cheap beads in a failed attempt to give it an American Indian look. Barbara Ham smiled at me, held up the sandal in her hand, screwed up her face in disgust and shook her head in mock displeasure.

The look on her face was hilarious, and I struggled to stifle a laugh.

Dave held up his cell phone for me to look at. There was a text from Emil that read, "The hot girl with the weird t-shirt says she's Drew girlfriend."

Ah ha, I thought. *That explains it.*

"Weird t-shirt?" I said to Dave. "That's sacrilege!"

Dave nodded in agreement. He had gone through a number of musical incarnations, including a serious punk rock phase when he was younger. He still had a healthy obsession with classic punk bands like The Clash, The Ramones and the Sex Pistols but his tastes spanned decades and genres. Although we talked about all kinds of music, we had immediately bonded over our love of the Beatles. Dave sometimes used his Beatle knowledge as a sort of litmus test for other employees. You were either in the club or you weren't, depending on your level of basic Beatle familiarity and, of course, the Beatles tunes or albums on your playlist. While it didn't impact one's ability to work at Ken's shoes, it did reflect your coolness level as far as Dave was concerned. Barbara Ham was wearing an Abbey Road t-shirt. That undoubtedly made her cool in Dave's eyes from the minute she walked into the door.

I looked up at the clock. I told Dave that I was going to take an early lunch, and that I might even be back late.

"Executive decision?" Dave asked.

"Yeah. Yeah, I guess it is," I replied.

He nodded his head as if he understood. "Rock on, man. No worries."

I marched over to where Barbara Ham was inspecting a slightly less horrific pair of summer sandals. She looked up as I approached.

"I have something to ask you," I began.

She straightened up, perhaps caught slightly off guard by the tone of my voice.

"Well," she said. "This sounds serious. Ask away."

"Chinese or Mexican?"

"I don't know. Are we talking about movies? Geopolitics? Pop culture? Drew, is this a trick question?"

"I was talking about food," I said.

"Aww," she said. "Food. That's excellent. I'm completely gut-foundered."

I had no idea what that meant, so I asked her how long she had to live.

"Gut-foundered," she explained, "means that I'm starving, at least in Canadian." She used her fingers to make the sign of quotation marks when she said the word Canadian. "You apparently did not listen to that part of your Rosetta Stone CD."

"Gut-foundered. Huh." I said, then I repeated the question, "Chinese or Mexican food?"

"Well," she continued, "I like them both of course. With Chinese you get a fortune cookie, and I always love getting some insight into the future. But with Mexican food you get tacos. And, let's face it, tacos, right?"

"How do you feel about tacos?" I asked.

She looked at me, held up a sandal like a microphone, and with an amazing amount of fake Whitney Houston gravitas, began to sing: *"I believe that tacos are our future, teach them well and let them lead the way, show them all the beauty they possess inside!"*

Her singing voice was actually very good, and she sang loudly enough to be heard by the other customers in the store. Jeff started to applaud, then realized he was alone in his admiration and stopped. Emil looked in our direction, scowled, and returned to selling shoes. I glanced over at Dave, who was still parked behind the register. He smiled and gave me a quick wink of approval.

Barbara Ham from Canada seemed unfazed. She looked at me and asked, "How do you feel about tacos, Drew?"

"I think it's safe to say that we are on the same page," I said, quickly adding, "Taco wise, I mean."

"Yes, taco wise indeed," she deadpanned, then raised her right arm up in a fisted salute. She gave me a quick nod to indicate that I was to do the same.

She's so...so...I don't know what, I thought, this person who I barely knew. I was immediately comfortable with her and that never happened. It was weird, but it was a good weird.

I followed suit and raised my arm. We stood there, in the middle of Ken's Shoes, each with a fist raised in a salute. I absolutely could not help it, and I looked again over at Emil on the other side of the sales floor. He stood there motionless, arms hanging at his sides, looking more baffled than ever.

I looked back at Barbara Ham. She was trying hard not to smile.

"Viva the taco revolution!" she said.

"Viva!" I echoed.

We put our arms down.

"Now that we are compadres, I was wondering if I could buy you lunch?" I asked her.

"Wow! These fake boyfriend benefits are really piling up. Sure."

We started to leave for lunch, passing Dave at the cash register, where I told him I was heading out. I added, "We're both gut-foundered," and smiled. "Apparently, that means really hungry in Canada," I explained.

Dave gave me a nod like he knew exactly what I was talking about, then returned his attention to the next customer he needed to ring up. Barbara Ham and I walked to the front door. I caught Emil's puzzled scowl as we left. He was still trying to wrap his head around the sudden appearance of my mystery girlfriend. It was amazing just how much I was enjoying his bewildered state.

Outside, it was a beautiful, nearly perfect, cloudless day. It was cool side, but there wasn't a trace of wind and I could smell the rich and unmistakable salty air of the ocean. It had been rainy earlier in the week, but the past few days had been great.

My freshman year I took a writing class where the professor taught us about committing a singular moment to memory. As a class exercise, we would try to memorize a moment in time and then write about it. It was harder than it sounds, but since then I had a habit of trying to mentally collect and file away any meaningful moment. Maybe it was the part of me that wanted to be a writer. I don't know. It didn't happen very often, but when a particular moment really stood out to me, I tried to bring it into razor-like focus and capture it. When it happened, I always felt as if I were on the outside of that split second looking in, and I tried very hard to remember it.

I looked over at the side of Barbara Ham's face. I sucked in some more of that salty air and took stock of my surroundings. I had made the short, two-minute walk to Taco Tyme countless times but today was different. I realized that I was beginning to think in the most boy-meets-girl clichéd way possible but I didn't care. This was different. The presence of this person I barely knew made it different, and I wanted to hold onto that moment if I could. I took a mental snapshot.

Barbara Ham noticed me looking at her and cocked her head questioningly. "What?" she asked.

"What do you mean, what?'" I retorted innocently.

"You just have a very suspicious look on your face," she said. "Like the cat who ate the canary. What's up with that? Did you eat the canary, Drew?"

I wasn't about to reveal to her that she was now part of my memory collection; that was well outside the border of any fake boyfriend territory and would just make me seem like some kind of freak or cybernetic Borg collective straight out of Star Trek. No, I wasn't going there.

"Tacos," I told her. "I was thinking about tacos."

She smiled, a little too knowingly, but said nothing.

We walked into Taco Tyme, a fake Spanish, mission-style building with the reinvented business name, and ordered our lunch. I paid, thankful for that twenty-dollar bill.

We sat down across from each other and ate. We talked to each other easily. We made each other laugh. I wanted to know about her and she happily chatted away. She had graduated in January from the University of British Columbia in Vancouver with a degree in business and a minor in French. After trying---not very hard she admitted---to find a job and feeling anxious to get out of her parents' home for a while, she decided to dedicate a year to visiting friends and relatives. She was on her way to Los Angeles to spend some time, probably the entire summer, with an aunt and uncle and a handful of her younger cousins. The uncle did "something" in the movie industry and apparently had boatloads of money.

"They have a huge pool," she said, "and the idea of lounging by the pool, in Los Angeles, and reading all of these books I want to read is so appealing. Did you ever just want to do nothing but read?" She asked.

"Yeah, like every day," I replied. I was pleased we both belonged to the I'd-rather-be-reading fellowship.

"Of course," she continued, "I may be bored to tears after two weeks. We'll see. What are you doing this summer?"

What was I doing this summer? I wasn't sure what I was doing on the weekend.

"Oh, you know," I began sarcastically. "Tennis lessons at the club, polo with the gang, sky diving when I get bored."

"Impressive." She played along. "What about Ken's Shoes? How will they live without you?"

"Don't worry," I said. "I'll stop in once in a while and check out my crew, just to make sure they're doing alright without me."

"How big of you to remember the little people," she teased.

I asked her about taking the bus from Canada to Los Angeles. "That seems like it would be a crazy long time on a bus." I said.

She rolled her eyes and said, "Tell me about it. From Vancouver, it's like two whole days to L.A.! I don't know what I was thinking. There's a car I can use when I get there and the idea of a long bus ride seemed like a good idea at the time. Stopping in all of these places, like here. Checking out the scenery. The Redwoods we drove through this morning were so beautiful. Honestly, it hasn't been that bad, but I would kill for a long, hot shower. I feel so grungy."

"Yeah," I said with a straight face, "I didn't want to say anything."

She smiled. "Oh, and you're a smart ass, too. Excellent."

I told her I really liked her t-shirt. I may have mentioned that Emil had called her t-shirt weird.

"Weird!" she exclaimed. "That's sacrilege!"

"Right? Those were my exact words! It is sacrilege!" I said. I mentioned that my mom sent me a music related t-shirt every year on my birthday, a traditional that began after I begged for a Green Day shirt for my tenth birthday. I had quite a few Beatle t-shirts as well, but not one with the Abbey Road cover.

Barbara lifted her soda cup, now filled with water, and I raised mine to meet it. We silently toasted to the excellence of the Beatles.

"How anyone could say that Abbey Road, the second-best Beatle album of all time, is weird is beyond me." She said, downright scoffing at the notion.

"Because the best Beatle album is Sgt. Pepper's, right?"

"Oh, I love Sgt. Peppers!" She went on, but in a very good English accent, "but no, luv, the best Beatle album is Revolver. Although they are all simply smashing!"

I did my best Ringo imitation. "I've got blisters on me fingers!"

"The White Album!" she exclaimed, her face lighting up. "Helter Skelter!"

She began to sing, her voice beautiful and edgy. *"When I get to the bottom, I go back to the top of the slide,"* she belted out.

I joined in, and we sang together: *"Where I stop and I turn and I go for a ride, till I get to the bottom and I see you again! Yeah, yeah, yeah."*

She stopped singing, but I carried on with the next line. *"Do you, don't you want me to love you?"* Ending at a near whisper when I realized she wasn't singing...and what I was saying. Yeah. Awkward.

We fell silent for what seem like an eternity, looking at each other and then looking away, only to look back at each other again.

She broke the silence. "Oh my God. I think we're turning lunch into Hallmark movie," she mused.

I wasn't sure how to interpret that. Was this saga going to have a happy ending? I didn't see how that was possible.

"Yeah, Hallmark movies. They're the worst," I said sarcastically.

I looked her, this intriguing enigma who had randomly walked into Ken's. I looked at that face and it was beautiful and flawless. I looked into her sparkling green eyes. I am now, I remember thinking, officially a basket case.

"Barbara Ham," I said.

"From Canada," she added.

Another moment of silence passed between us, neither of us sure of what to say next, not that it mattered. It was a good silence, then Barbara Ham broke it.

"Enough about me. What about you, Drew? As you Yanks like to say, what's your deal?'"

I told her I was an English Lit major and one day, I was going to write the great American novel. I also mentioned my screenplay about zombies.

"Zombies? Isn't everybody doing zombies?" she asked sardonically. "I think you're about 15 years behind the zombie curve."

I almost launched into an explanation of why my zombie screenplay, a story about a band of four punk rockers who die but come back to life to play again, would be original and hilarious, but I didn't. Instead I gave her the Reader's Digest, 100-words-or-less, easy-to-read type, version of my life. My normal, middle-class upbringing with my parents and younger sister. My drama-free school years. My less-than-inspiring high school years. My great high school English teacher, Mrs. Felton, who inspired me to read everything, and write.

Barbara told me that she was an only child, having been a surprise baby to her parents when they were both in their early forties. She had also had a reasonably, drama-free childhood and had grown up wanting to be singer in a band, something she said that she had accomplished in high school with a band she founded.

"You may have heard of us," she said teasingly. "Silver Slugs North. Ring a bell? No? We were a big hit at Jenny Carlson's seventeenth birthday party. Sadly, we disbanded shortly after that."

"Creative control issues?" I guessed.

"Boys," She answered wryly and rolled her eyes.

We talked for almost another hour. Dave was going to kill me. Emil was going to have a field day. I didn't care. Talking to her was easy, as if we had been friends for a long time. We liked a lot of the same things, having similar taste in books, music, and movies. We also got sidelined and talked about more serious stuff like politics and global warming.

Barbara smiled brightly and said, "Drew, you are so much deeper than you look!"

I told her that I spent a lot of my free time thinking deep thoughts. Just for pondering's sake, I added. She said that was apparent and laughed.

We shifted gears and talked about where we had travelled, and where we would like to go. Both of us agreed that a few months backpacking in Europe would be awesome. As we talked, I was keenly aware of the electricity I was feeling between us. I wondered if she was feeling anything remotely similar.

Barbara glanced at her cell phone. "Oh shit!" She said, and abruptly stood from her chair.

Alarmed, I stood up with her. "What's the matter?"

"My bus is leaving is fifteen minutes. I need to get over there."

We walked out and stopped in front of the restaurant. I knew parting was inevitable, but it still sucked. It felt weird to realize I was losing my love-at-first-sight fake girlfriend, particularly since I had never even believed in love at first sight. My last couple of serious girlfriends (serious girlfriends? what does that even mean?) had begun as casual acquaintances who became friends, who became girlfriends. Those relationships both ended with a mutually amicable fizzling out, where I went my way and they went theirs, lost in an ocean of backpacks and academia.

I looked at her face, those freckles and the smile that was trying very hard not to become lopsided. I realized that we didn't know each, and that the truth was we were really nothing but people who barely knew each other. A random meeting. A long lunch. Nothing. The part that stung, I thought, was that I was losing the promise of what could be.

"Barbara Ham. From Canada," I started.

"Drew, you don't know me. I mean, not really," she said, still trying to hold her smile.

"Stop," I said.

She put a single, index finger up to my lips.

"I binge watch reality TV," She said. "I mean for hours at time. It's horrible, but there you go."

"Barbara," I tried again. She stopped me.

"I am addicted to claw machines. Seriously. I can't help myself. I see a claw machine and I have to try it. It's a sickness, and I'm hooked. I have spent hundreds of dollars and have virtually nothing to show for it. I'm an addict, Drew. I know I need help."

"Seriously," I said softly. "Stop it."

"Oh wait! And, I'm a shoplifter!" she blurted out. "I have stolen things from a store. There you go. Absolutely no moral character whatsoever."

"Really?" I asked skeptically.

"Absolutely" She said.

"And when was this, exactly?"

She pursed her lips and avoided my eyes.

"Seriously, when?" I prodded.

"OK, OK," she said. "I was five. I took some Pop Rocks out of the store. My mom caught me and marched me right back in to apologize to the manager. It's on my record, I'm pretty sure."

"Whoa! What a minute," I said, "*Taste the explosion*, Pop Rocks?" making the quotation sign in the air with my hands

She nodded. I liked her more and more, but I really didn't get her attempt to persuade me otherwise and I said so.

"Why are you trying so hard to convince me you're a giant pain in the ass?" I said. "I like you. I don't want you to leave. I want you to stay. I want to get to know you."

She started to say something, but I cut her off.

"Don't get on that bus. Hang out with me. No strings. No anything. Go tomorrow, or in a couple of days." I checked the date on my watch. "And in three weeks, if by some phenomenon you are still around, you could take me out for my birthday. I'm thinking tacos."

She smiled. "My birthday is in a month, so like a week later than yours." She sang softly, *"They say it's your birthday, it's my birthday too, yeah."*

I continued. "It's crazy, I get it, but I like you. You're funny and smart and have great taste in music. Obviously."

She pointed to the front of her t-shirt. "Obviously," she agreed with a slight eye roll.

"Plus, you're OK looking," I said.

She reached up and pulled my face close to hers. Then she gave me a quick, soft kiss on my lips. It wasn't the kiss of a new beginning, it was the kiss of a sad goodbye.

"Drew, listen to me," she started. "You're lovely. Such a nice, sweet guy. So funny. And with nearly impeccable taste in music."

"But" I said, leaving it out there, dangling between us.

"But, I just got out of a relationship with someone. And now I need something more than cute, nice and funny. Do you know why I broke it off with him?"

Of course I didn't. "No discount on shoes?" I joked half-heartedly.

"No, Drew. It's because I realized that there needs to be…" she trailed off.

"What?" I asked. "Needs to be what?"

"God, you're going to think I'm crazy. I just think…I just need… there needs to be a something else. Something like a romantic epiphany, or a sense that the stars have aligned. There needs to be something other than boy meets girl or girl meets boy. I know how that sounds, Drew, I do. Please don't be mad." She paused and said, "I want to be Paul and Linda. I don't want to be John and Cynthia. Does that make sense?"

I got the Beatle reference of course, but I said, "No." I didn't know what she was trying to tell me. I really didn't know what she wanted. Fireworks? A marching band? Some sort of cinematic, rom-com twist?

"Listen," I told her, "You can just tell me the truth. If you don't like me--"

"Don't like you?" she interrupted. "Don't like you? Drew, oh my God, of course I like you! Do you think I'm crazy to want some sort of cosmic confirmation?"

"A little bit, yes." I said. "What do you want, Barbara? Thunderbolts and lightning? Cupid's arrow?"

"Something like that," she said softly. "I'm not crazy. I'm not. I just know what I want, I guess."

I was hurt. I was confused. But it wasn't an outright rejection so I suppose I was also hopeful. But she wanted a sign and I had nothing. What does that even mean, I wondered. How would I even know what I was looking for? I asked her.

She leaned in close to me. "You'll know. I trust you to know. Now hand me your phone."

She took my phone and quickly put her name and Los Angeles address in my contacts.

"What about your phone number?" I asked.

She smiled. "Send me a postcard for now." She checked the time again. "Shit!" she exclaimed.

Without another word, she turned and jogged off in the direction of the bus station. I watched her until she disappeared around a corner. Now it was my turn to say, "Shit." I looked for a few more moments in that direction, then I walked slowly back to work. Dave must have seen the look on my face because he didn't say a word as I walked in. Even Emil seemed wary and, at least for the rest of the day, gave me no additional grief. Jeff ambled by and asked me what happened to my girlfriend.

"She had to go," I said simply.

The next couple of weeks were pure crap. It started raining again and didn't let up. That was fine; it matched my mood. Each day, I dragged myself to class, and then I dragged myself to work. Emil reverted true to form and was particularly prickly. I told Dave the whole Barbara-Ham-from-Canada story, a confessional that took place in his office one day before closing while we listened to an old Boston album. I watched that record slowly spin on the turntable, the needle gently bobbing on that black disk, just going around and around and around. I could relate. Christ, what a mind numbingly, pathetic, sad sack of a person I was becoming. It should've been comical, a funny story you could tell your friends, except it wasn't.

When I told Dave about my lunch with Barbara Ham, I said that I had asked her to stay, but she hadn't. I mentioned that she needed something, a sign.

"A sign?" Dave asked. "What kind of sign?"

"Yes," I said. "Exactly. I have been asking myself that very question."

"She's from Canada," He said. "That may be the problem."

"Yes, she is from Canada but, no, that is not the problem."

He paused, and then said, "Justin Bieber is from Canada."

Wow, I thought. A little exasperated, I sighed out a "Really?" and added, "But, so is Neil Young."

"That's true," Dave said. "But so is Nickelback."

Maybe he was trying to make me feel better; I knew better than to think Dave had anything against Canadian musicians or bands. I also knew how to end the conversation.

"Let me think for a minute," I started, then I rattled off as many Canadian bands or musicians as I could think of off the top of my head. "Drake, Rush, Arcade Fire, The Weekend, Bryan Adams and, and that band that sang "American Women," I'm pretty sure they were Canadian."

"The Guess Who," Dave said.

"Yes!" I said, "Yes. The Guess Who. Oh, and what about The Band? Come on, The Band, The Last Waltz! They were from Canada, right?" A few months previously Dave had put the Martin Scorsese directed documentary, filmed twenty years before I was born, on my list to further my rock and roll education. It did, and was excellent.

"Not the drummer," he said. "Levon Helm was American." He looked up at the ceiling and said, "R.I.P., brother!"

Our conversation ended with Dave suggesting that I would eventually get over it. He was probably right, but for the first time in my life I felt as if fate had conspired against me, ironic because just like love at first sight, I didn't believe in fate either. I had always been more of a hap and circumstance kind of guy, but I would happily have gone with fate if Barbara Ham from mother-flipping Canada would have stayed.

Despite my best efforts, I thought about her all the time. At one point I even Googled her, finding only bits and pieces of dated social media posts. I also Googled the address of house where she was staying in Los Angeles. It was enormous and expensive looking. I began to feel a little bit like a voyeuristic creep and stopped searching altogether. I did send her a postcard a couple of times, always jotting something that I thought she would find funny.

The following Saturday I worked a full shift and tried to enthusiastically get back to the business of selling shoes. Jorge and Jeff were both working. Emil, thankfully, had the day off. Dave was playing music by a Seattle band I had never heard of, Tacocat, and their jangly, upbeat pop filled the store which, despite the current overcast, made it feel like a true prelude to the upcoming summer. Sandals, sneakers and open toe heels flew off the shelves, and the three of us, along with Dave, stayed busy until closing.

I drove the 15-minutes back to my apartment in silence. I didn't bother to turn on the radio or play any music off my phone; I didn't have a playlist that matched my mood.

When I got home, my roommate Rusty was on the couch watching something on Netflix. He greeted me with, "Monica's here," referring to my other roommate Brian's girlfriend, who in past three months had become a semi-permanent fixture at the apartment. As Rusty and Brian had shared a bedroom, Monica's presence relegated Rusty to the sofa, but he never seemed to mind. I was glad that I had won the rock, paper, scissors showdown when we signed the lease, and gotten the smaller second bedroom to myself.

The next few days seemed to move forward in slow motion. I had a rare Sunday off and spent the entire day reading. I re-read J.D. Salinger's short story, *The Laughing Man*, a story about a relationship that waxes and then wanes away, which struck me as extremely fitting given my general state of emotional funkiness. I had a sudden urge to send a copy to Barbara Ham with a note saying, "See! This is what you've done to me!" followed by a sad face or two. I immediately realized how pitiful that would be and mentally backspaced over the very thought of it. Still in the mood to read, I grabbed my tablet and tore through the novel *Ready Player One*, a former bestseller which had been on my list to read since high school. It proved to be entertaining, even if I didn't get all of the 1980s pop culture references. For a while, at least, it took my mind off all the other stuff.

The week ahead would bring both my last day of class and my birthday for which I didn't have any real plans. Normally, I would drive the five hours home to spend the weekend and do copious amounts of laundry, but my parents were on vacation in Cancun for another week. My default plan had been to go out with my roommates, but Brian and Monica were acting like an old married couple, which made bar hopping a lot less adventurous than it had been in the pre-Monica days.

The week prodded on. The last day of class was a relief. I was still waiting for one exam score, but I was fairly sure I had done well. I contemplated, briefly, taking a summer school class, but scrapped the idea and decided that I would just work, read, write and hang out. Dave said he could give me more hours during the summer if I hung around, which I planned to do after a quick trip back home. To say my summer plans were flexible was an understatement. I wasn't feeling particularly ambitious, although I wanted to finally get to work on my screenplay and get through some of the required reading for the fall term, potentially my last at school if I got my shit together.

I woke up late Friday morning, my birthday, to the sounds of bedsprings and the rhythmic thumping of the Ikea headboard against the wall in the adjoining bedroom; Brian and Monica were acting like a not-so-old married couple. I wanted to shout out "get a room!" but was sure the irony would have been lost. Instead, I booted up my laptop, put on my headphones and checked what was going on in the world while listening to Lily Allen, my unrequited musical love. I had a lot happy birthday messages from friends and family, including a video from my little sister and a few of her fellow high school senior friends. Very random, but funny. She could be, as my mom would say, "a real goofball."

I wasn't scheduled to work at Ken's until 1:00 PM, so I killed time on my laptop because nothing kills time like randomly crisscrossing the great world-wide-web and bouncing off the walls of a seemingly endless cyberspace. A couple of hours later, I emerged from my room in search of food.

Rusty, as always, was lounging on the sofa. "Hey," he said looking up, "this came for you." He handed me a large, padded envelope. It was from my mom. The t-shirt tradition continued. I opened it up.

In hindsight, I didn't know that was the first sign, the initial star rattling and clanking its way, like a lotto ball, to the first-in-line position. How could I have known that? I just thought it was an amazing coincidence. I pulled out the t-shirt. It features a picture of the Beatles Abbey Road album cover on it. There they were, the Fab Four---Paul without shoes---strolling across that street 50 years prior. It was identical to one that Barbara Ham had worn.

"NO! WAY!" I hollered, articulating each word, loud enough to make Rusty sit up straight.

"Hey," he said, "What the Hell?"

Brian poked his head out of his room. "Dude, what happened?" he asked, scanning the room, looking for the source of my outburst.

"Nothing," I said, "Nothing. Sorry."

I forgot I was hungry and decided just to get ready for work. I jumped in and out of the shower, slapped on some deodorant, pulled on my new the t-shirt and left. Not exactly dress code, but whatever.

The weather had changed from gloomy to bright sunshine, and I drove to work with the window down and the radio blasting. I arrived at Ken's early, a rarity for me, and thought I would just go in and B.S. with Dave for a while. If it was busy he might even tell me to clock in, which was fine with me. I locked my car and went into the store.

As I stepped inside, Emil was just emerging from the back room. He spotted me and made a beeline in my direction, grinning from ear-to-ear. He looked happy to see me and that caught me completely off guard. As he reached me I flinched a little, not sure it I was going to get sucker punched or not. But Emil reached out me and grabbed me into a big bear hug.

What the hell? I thought, my arms dangling down by my side. *Seriously, what the hell?* I thought as Emil released me from his grasp and stepped back, still grinning like a mad man.

"Drew!" he exclaimed. "Hey! How's it going? Good to see you!"

I pulled back even further and looked him in the eye. If he was screwing with me, I couldn't tell.

"Are you screwing around with me right now?" I asked him.

He threw his head back and laughed.

"Come on," he said. "I want to show you something." Then he herded me back out of the store to the far end of the parking lot. I almost couldn't keep up with him as he practically dragged me along.

When we got there, he didn't say a word. He just pointed. There, parked on an angle and taking up two spaces, was a jet-black Corvette. It was immaculate and truly a beautiful machine. Emil was beaming like a new father. I had never, ever seen him like this. It was surreal. But I could see why he was so happy. He finally had managed to get the car he always wanted. I don't know how many thousands of shoes he had to sell to make it happen, but I was happy for him.

"That," I told him with all sincerity, "is a bad ass automobile."

"I know, right!" he said. "It's a 2013 Z06. Seven-liter V8. Over 500 horsepower. And, it only has twenty-five thousand miles on it. Can you believe it?"

I asked him if it had belonged to some little, old lady who only drove it to church. He laughed maniacally. "Hey, that's funny!"

We stood there for another moment, both gazing admiringly at the Corvette. I mumbled something about getting back to work and started to head back to the store.

"Hey, Drew," he shouted out from behind me, making me stop and look back, "I'm sorry if I'm an asshole sometimes."

I wasn't sure it I had heard him correctly. I turned and took a step back in his direction. "What?"

He shrugged, looking slightly embarrassed. "I know I can be a prick. Sorry. Oh yeah, and happy birthday!"

"Thanks." I said. The fact that he knew it was my birthday made the moment even stranger, if that were even possible.

He nodded, and with that I turned and headed back to the store. Well, I thought, I did not see that coming.

Walking in, I saw that both Jeff and Jorge were out on the floor, although the store didn't have any customers at the moment. There were also no signs of Dave. Jeff walked by and said, "Hey man, Happy Birthday. Cool shirt."

Seriously? I thought.

Jeff and Jorge were picking up boxes of shoes. I was getting ready to find something to do when the door opened behind me. I turned around. It was Drizella, smiling happily as she gave me a little wave.

"I just thought I would stop by to see if you had anything new in stock."

We both knew the drill, so I asked her to sit down while I checked. Already a few steps away, I remembered something and circled around back to her.

"I'm sorry," I apologized, "but I was just wondering what your name is. I mean, you come in all the time and I just thought I would ask."

She smiled. "It's Ella," she said.

Ella? She practically was a Drizella! I wondered if Emil, the creator of the Drizella moniker, knew it was her real name. I went to the back. We got our shipments on Thursday, so anything new would be on the shelves. We had quite a few new styles I noticed, something that Dave said would happen as we got closer to Summer.

Like love at first sight and fate, I didn't believe in miracles either. But every time Ella showed up at Ken's I secretly wished for one. Just once I wanted to find something nice in her size. Just once I wanted her cheery optimism to be validated. Just once I wanted to really find her perfect fit. Just once, I always thought. That day, I found a pair of really nice flats, a pair of fashionable sandals and some tennis shoes all in her size. Ella tried each pair on and, miracles of miracles, each pair fit perfectly.

"Oh, my gosh!" she said, "I'm so happy!" I was, too. Emil, now manning the register and still beaming, rang up the sale. As she left Emil called out, "Thanks for shopping at Ken's Shoes, Ella! See you next time."

Jorge came up to me and asked me if it was really my birthday. I told him it was actually alternate universe Friday.

"I don't know what that means," He said, "but Feliz Cumpleaños, brother."

I asked him where Dave was. Jorge said that he had been there, but that he had hustled out of the store about an hour before, saying he would be back. He added, "Did you see Emil's new car? Cool, isn't it?" I agreed. It was way cool.

Just then, Dave flew into the store carrying a plastic bag and out of breath.

He saw me and shouted, "Drew! Drew!" before he turned and ran towards his office. Midway there, he stopped and did a hard pivot. "Drew, come here!" he beckoned. He took another step towards his office and then spun around again as if he couldn't decide where to go. He put his hand back up and said, "No, wait! Wait there!" He did a quick double take and added, randomly, "Hey, I like that shirt!" Then he disappeared into his office. Crazy.

A few seconds passed. Then, unbelievably, the unmistakable first chords of the classic Clash song came pounding out of the stores' PA system, cranked up to max. It was surreal and I was speechless, locked in place as the first few lines came booming out.

Darlin' you got to let me know

Should I stay or should I go?

If you say that you are mine

I'll be here 'til the end of time

So you got to let me know

Should I stay or should I go?

Dave came out of his office, bouncing around violently like he was in the middle of a mosh pit. He was beaming, laughing and then he belted out the first part of the song at the top of his lungs. He turned to me and shouted, "Can you believe it? I found it! It's practically new! It's perfect!" Jeff and Jorge also got the bug and started dancing around the store. Even Emil was happily bobbing his head. I was glad the store was empty, although I don't think it would have mattered.

Suddenly, all the synapses in my brain began exploding in sync.

Barbara Ham from Canada said that she wanted there to be a sign. I began the checklist in my head. My new t-shirt (check), Emil getting his 'Vette and turning into Mr. nice guy (check), Ella finding her shoes (check), Dave finding the album of his dreams (check). Everyone was getting what they wanted. Everybody. The song came back around to the line, "Should I stay or should I go?"

Then it hit me hard. I should go. I had to go. This was as close to the stars aligning as I was going to get. This was it, I thought. This had to be it, right? I decided that, oh Hell yes, this was it. I ran to the back to grab my keys. I dashed back out to the sales floor and grabbed Dave by the shoulders. "Dave!" I shouted to be heard over the music. Dave held up a finger to signal I was to wait, then jogged back to his office. The volume of the music came down and Dave came back out.

"Crazy, right?" he said, still grinning.

"Yeah, crazy." I replied. "Listen, I need to go. I'm really sorry. Can you take me off the schedule for a while?"

"Sure," he said. "Where are you going?"

I told him. Then I asked him how long it he thought it would take to get there. He scratched his head. "I don't know for sure, but ten or eleven hours at least." I did the math in my head. It was about 1:30. If I left now, I could pull over and sleep for a few hours, arriving in L.A. in the early morning. Barbara was staying in San Marino, wherever that was. I had an address. I had my phone. With some help from Google Maps I would find it, and when I got there I would camp out on that doorstep. She said I would know, and I knew.

Dave motioned Jeff and Jorge over. Emil started to come over as well, but a customer walked in and, of course, he grabbed him. Some things would never change.

Dave told Jeff and Jorge that I was going to be taking off. "But," he said, "We found out it was your birthday, so we got you a little something." He disappeared into his office, and can back out with a wrapped present, which he handed to me. It was unexpected. I opened it, and found it was actually two gifts. A hard copy book of the *Casablanca* screenplay (Dave knew I was a fan), and a CD by a band called The Crunch, 'Brand New Brand.' Dave said, "They're good, even on a CD. I'm still looking for the album for you."

I said thanks, and told Dave I would let him know what was going with me as soon as I knew. I said goodbye to the guys, Emil gave me a thumbs up from the other side of the store; maybe he wasn't such a prick after all. I pulled my keys out of my pocket.

Dave slapped his forehead. "Oh man, I almost forgot, something came for you." He went back to his office. I was jonesing to get out of there and hit the road. Dave returned and handed me an envelope.

The postmark was from Los Angeles. I tore it open. Inside was a handmade birthday card. The front featured a hand drawn taco. I muffled a laugh. Inside it, she had written, "It's your birthday? You GUAC to be kidding me! Can I buy you a taco?"

That was funny, I thought. Suddenly, I had a thought. Could she buy me a taco? She was asking if she could buy me a taco. I looked at Dave.

"I know you just got here," he said sheepishly, "but if you wanted to go and get something to eat, that's cool with me." He looked at Jeff and Jorge, "Are you guys okay with Drew taking a lunch now?"

Jeff nodded, a little too enthusiastically, and said he had no problem with that. Jorge echoed the same thing, in Spanish, "vete a comer!" There were dots, lots of dots, but I was still not connecting all of them.

"I mean," Dave said, "you should probably only go eat if you're gut-foundered."

The proverbial light exploded over my head. A switched flipped in my brain. I looked at the three co-conspirators, each with a pathetic Cheshire cat grin. I shook my head at them, then I bolted out of the store. I sprinted across the parking lot and into the street, not even bothering to look both ways. I got to Taco Tyme in record time, bursting through the door, arms pin-wheeling to keep my balance.

She was sitting at a table, our table I couldn't help thinking. A hard laugh erupted from the bottom of my throat. I had so many things I wanted to ask her, so many things I wanted to tell her, including the amazing events of the day, but I was too stunned and overwhelmed that she was really there, beautiful and smiling. I didn't understand anything. I stood there, dumbfounded, unable to speak. There were just too much stuff flooding my brain, but none of it was making it out of my mouth. She was here. Crazy. So crazy. Happy, happy birthday to me.

Barbara Ham from Canada stood up and took the three strides that brought her face mere inches from mine. She was beaming, her green eyes filled with laughter. She leaned forward and kissed me lightly on the lips, then put her mouth next to my ear.

"Hey you," she whispered, "I like your shirt."

THE END

The Coldest Shower in Morocco

Another travel story
By Jon Waldrep

This morning I had to re-light the pilot light in the water heater, so the shower I ended up taking was on the cold side. I survived, but it reminded me of something that happened several years ago.

In my 20s, I lived in Spain for a number of years. That first year, living in the capital city of Madrid, I made a wide and eclectic assortment of friends. Mark was a tall, British guy who worked in the same language school that I did, teaching English to bored school-aged kids and some, slightly more enthusiastic, young adults. We became good friends and celebrated drinking buddies. I refer to that first year in Madrid, in my best Lennonesque, as my 'lost weekend.' Mark and I and an assorted cast of characters went out almost every night, starting most nights at the Casa de la Cerveza, a short walk from the Bilbao metro station. The Casa de la Cerveza was not unlike thousands of other bars in Madrid, offering an assortment of cheap beer and an excellent variety of tapas and other food. The real attraction of the place, as far as we were concerned, was the arm wrestling bartender. After getting a beer and a tapa, Mark would egg me on to arm wrestle the bartender which, despite my uninspiring record of no wins, no losses and 100% draws, I almost always did. I might have taken solace in that record if the bartender had been a hulking, middle-linebacker type with biceps the size of summer melons. But no, the arm wrestling bartender at the Casa de la Cerveza was maybe 5' 7" and 135 pounds soaking wet and looked more like an unassuming accountant than a local arm wrestling champion. I learned with each successive encounter that, despite his size, he was strong as hell and it took everything I had just to keep my knuckles off the counter.

Another friend I made early on in Madrid was Sophia, a spirited Greek girl who lived in the same dilapidated residencia that I did. The old building was on a small street that curved up from the Plaza de Isabel II and the Opera metro station to near the Gran Via, one of Madrid's main arteries and right in the heart of the Spanish capital. Sophia was an outgoing social butterfly who lived to go out and dance and was a fixture in the surrounding discos and dance clubs. Occasionally she would drag me along despite my protests that I didn't dance. "It doesn't matter," she would say, "You can watch me! And if I want to get rid of a guy I don't like you can pretend to be my boyfriend!" That was a skillset I could get my arms around, so I spent a few nights a month watching Sophia dance with reckless abandon to whatever ear-splitting dance hit was popular at the moment. Occasionally I would find myself tapping some guy on the shoulder, telling him to move along and fill his dance card somewhere else.

Anna was an American who was just hanging out in Madrid for an undetermined amount of time until she decided to move on or she ran out of money and went back home to Chicago. She and I had met in front of a bar where I had tried, shamelessly, to convince her to immediately dump her Spanish boyfriend for me. This was particularly awkward as he was standing right there next to her. "¿Qué está diciendo?

(What's he saying?) he asked her, more than once, muttering it under his breath while looking at me suspiciously. "Nothing," she said, "He's just being silly," she replied in Spanish. The irony of wanting to say, "Hey! I'm standing right here," was not lost on me. After several minutes of my best sidewalk banter, I realized I was not going to prevail. Anna gave me an A-for-effort smile and walked off with her Spanish boyfriend, sending me a sardonic wink while the boyfriend offered me a cocky, yet confused, stare down. I had managed to get Anna's address, so that same night I wrote her a long, epic, what I hoped was funny, letter which I ended with, "We'll always have that time, on the sidewalk, in front of that bar, with what's his name. Don't ever forget that." In the end, that letter prompted us to stay in touch and eventually become friends. It also encouraged her to say to me, "You should be a writer," but I told I wasn't ready to give up my dreams of being an NBA point guard.

Days of teaching English and nights of practically dislocating my arm at the Casa de la Cerveza passed. Our group of friends spent most nights together and often hopped on a bus or train for a weekend jaunt outside of Madrid. When Semana Santa (Easter break) rolled around Mark and I decided to go to Morocco for a week. When Sophia found out a few days later she knocked on my door in the residencia. "You guys are going to Morocco?" she asked. I confirmed that we were. "Well, I'm going, too," she said. The more the merrier I told her, and it was settled. Anna did just about the same thing later that week, so then we were four. It was a little odd, because none of us were boyfriend and girlfriend, but we all liked each other and got along well so we decided it was a good mix. "Besides," Anna said at one point, "everyone brings something to the table." I'm not sure what I brought, except the ability to drive a stick shift and the questionable skill of warding off unwelcomed advances, but I accepted Anna's proclamation at face value.

We met at the Atocha Train Station and caught the overnight train that would take us from Madrid to southern tip of Spain and the city of Algeciras. Sophia had a small boom box, and we listened to a cassette of Madonna's 'Like a Virgin' ad nauseam as the train chugged slowly along. I finally proclaimed that I had been touched way past the very first time, and begged Sophia to give it a rest. The train took us into the darkness and we did the best we could to get comfortable and sleep. The next morning, we took a ferry across the Strait of Gibraltar to Tangiers. The smell of the ocean was invigorating and we enjoyed the hour-and-a-half ride across the strait of Gibraltar. When we arrived in Tangiers, we were greeted with the usual throng of people who wanted to carry our bags or get us a taxi or take us to a hotel. A friend of mine from Iran, also living in Madrid, had taught me the one and only word he claimed I would need in Arabic, "La" meaning 'no.' We la la la'd our way to the car rental agency, where I signed a bunch of papers and rented us a car. It was a Renault 4, a little, boxy French toy of a car with a stick shift that stuck out from under the dashboard and curled up like a hat rack. It took me a minute or two of gear grinding to figure out how to shift it, but then I pretty much had it.

As anyone who has ever been to Tangiers will tell you, the best thing about Tangiers is getting out of Tangiers and we wasted no time throwing our backpacks into the back of the Renault and hitting the road. Driving in Tangiers, or just about any Moroccan city, meant deftly negotiating narrow streets and roundabouts filled with not only cars and trucks, but also hordes of bicycles, scooters and the occasional farm animal. I managed to get us out the city intact, with only a few shaking fists from the locals, as I piloted our little Renault, bobbing and weaving our way through traffic until we were on the highway heading out of town.

The week before we had loosely planned our trip with the help of a tattered and dog-eared copy of a Spain, Portugal & Morocco 'Let's Go' guidebook that I had bought in California before I left for Spain. We had decided to spend the first night of our trip in a very small village at the base of the Rif mountain range, not far from the city of Quezzan. We arrived at the hostel in the late afternoon. The snow on the mountain tops in the distance made for a picturesque background, and the air was much chillier than it had been in Tangiers.

The guidebook had not lied about the hostel being bare-boned. It was barer than bare-boned, but it cost the equivalent of about $10 for all four of us and after a long day of travel we were tired, hungry and grimy and not very picky about our accommodations. The old women who ran the place walked us to our room, chatting away to no one in particular in Berber or Moroccan Arabic or another language none of us understood a word of. It became apparent that except for a very few words, she didn't speak English, Spanish or even French, any one of which someone in our group could have handled. In the northern part of Morocco, you can normally manage with Spanish and English, further south it's French and English, but she hadn't gotten that memo. That was fine, each of us just wanted a place to drop our stuff, a meal somewhere and a bed. After checking in, basically just logging our names in a large guest book, I remember thinking it was odd that she hadn't grabbed a room key from the small table that served as her front desk. When I saw the room, it made more sense. There was no door. No door, no curtain, nothing but a framed doorway where a door might had been once. The women shuttled us into the large room and we looked around. It looked like an abandoned hospital room, or the world's worst summer camp, with four, ancient single beds lined up against the wall. There wasn't a window or any other furnishings. My room in the residencia back in Madrid was nothing special but was palatial compared to this place. I reasoned that it was about $2.50 for me for the night and couldn't complain, but the others looked doubtful.

We poked around and determined that the communal bathroom was across the way and a shower room was available at the end of the long hallway. Anna finally said that she wasn't staying in a room without a door. We could see her point. We asked the women, in assorted languages, if we could get a room with a door. She looked at us like we were speaking Greek. Sophia may have actually been speaking Greek, I don't remember, but you get the idea. The old, Moroccan women however did not get the idea. We pantomimed the door. Nothing. I pretended to be a door, with Mark opening and closing me. I even provided the appropriate door squeaking sound, still nothing. We were about to give up when the figurative light bulb went off over the women's head. I don't speak Berber or Arabic, but I can state with near certainty that she said, "Oh! A door! You want a door! Of course!" She made a motion for us to stay put and went off to resolve the problem. "Jon," Sophia said, "you're actually a very good door impersonator." I thanked her and made a mental note to add that to my list of special skills.

A few minutes later we heard someone making a quite a racket and heading in our direction. Moments later the women appeared, struggling as she dragged a door behind her. She smiled at us, triumphant. The door didn't fit the room's door frame, but we leaned it up against the door frame from the inside and all decided that, for one night, it would suffice. Anyone sneaking into our room would knock it over and make a lot of noise, so at least we would be killed fully awake. We went out to find something to eat, taking our backpacks with us as a precaution, and found a little café not far from the hostel. I joked that I wanted to look for a 'Berger King' for dinner and then go find a TV where we could watch a re-run of 'Leave it to Berber,' and got a couple of collective groans for my efforts. After a meal and a couple of mint teas, we returned to the hostel. With our misfit door propped up into position, we all collapsed and slept like the dead.

The next morning I woke up first. The door was still in place and my throat was un-slit. Both, I though, pretty good signs. The morning air was really cold and the building was unheated and drafty, so even without windows our room felt like the inside of a Coleman Cooler. I stood up from bed and could feel cold puffs of air swirl around my ankles like an emotionally needy cat looking for attention. I was desperate to take a shower and wash away the grunge of the last 24 hours, so I gathered up some clean clothes and my meager bathroom supplies and went down the long hallway to the shower room. It was surprising how big it was. The room was a large circle, easily 15 feet in diameter. The shower head was at the end of a long section of pipe that came down to the center of the room from the high ceiling. A chain with a handle hung off of the shower head, the on-and-off mechanism I assumed. I took off my clothes and piled them on top of the cement and tile bench that jutted out from one part of the wall. The shower room, like the rest of the place, was freezing. I could see my breath as I walked to the center of it, soap in hand. I positioned myself under the shower head and pulled down on the chain. The moment the water hit me I had to stifle a scream, and a long list of very specific obscenities. Son of a fill-in-the-blank! The water that poured down on me in a deluge was so cold that for a moment I didn't know if I was being frozen to death or scalded alive. It took a second to realize it was the former. Saying the water was cold was an understatement. The water was crazy, ice forming, testicle inverting, heart-attack inducing, mind-numbingly cold. I let go of the chain handle and stood there in that very cold room, wet from that dreadfully icy water. My teeth were chattering and I shivered uncontrollably. Now what? My brain was too frozen to think straight. I felt like I had just downed a Big Gulp sized Slurpee while taking a bath in ice water. I debated what to do, then quickly made a decision.

Did you ever run out of milk as a kid and convince yourself that you could use water on your Frosted Flakes or Count Chocula and just pretend it was fine? Sort of a Matrix inspired mind-over-matter technique in which if you believed it, it was true? It was with that woolly-headed resolve that I decided I was going to take that shower and that it would be fine. Just fine. Nothing to see here folks, just a guy taking a shower. Mind over matter. I inched my near frozen body back into position under that shower head. I realized that the quirky thing about the shower was that you had to be standing directly under the shower head, and freezing water, to pull the chain. There was no way to stand off to the side, away from the water and then pull the chain with the remote hope that the water would warm up. Nope. With this shower you were all in, all-or-nothing, make or break. I braced myself and pulled the chain. The freezing cold water poured down. I held my breath as my body clenched up. After a few seconds I let go of the chain and grabbed my bar of soap. I soaped up every part of my body in record time, using a high speed, herky-jerk motion. Anyone watching would have thought that I was having a seizure, while impressively remaining upright. I pulled the dreaded handle once more and let that freezing water pour over me just long enough to rinse the soap off and turn my skin color a lovely shade of cornflower blue. I walked away from the middle of the room, my body shaking violently. Had I ever been this cold before? I had taken cold showers before. I had taken showers in cold rooms. But never had I done both and certainly not to this extreme. I dried off with one of the threadbare towels stacked neatly on the end of the bench, my hands shaking, impossibly trying to warm up. I got into my clothes and goose-stepped myself back down the hall, flailing my arms around to find my long, lost circulation. I'm not sure what I must have looked like. A zombie suffering a massive Tourette's attack? A mummy awakened from the dead? A kid fighting my way down a hallway filled with spider webs? It could not have been pretty.

When I got back to the room the others were just waking up. I had recovered, for the most part, but still felt cold and shivered sporadically. Mark sat up in the bed. "Did you take a shower?" he asked me. "How was it?" Did he not see I was still slightly blue? Could he not tell I was shivering in my clothes? Alright, I thought. This is what they mean when they say to make the best of a bad situation. I gave him my best, broadest, most infectious, happy grin, pressing my teeth together so they wouldn't chatter, and with the cheerful enthusiasm of a middle school cheerleader I said, "It was awesome!" "Right," he said, getting up, gathering some things and tottering off in the direction of the shower room. "Hey" I said as he was walking out of the room, "Just an FYI, it's kind of cold when you start, and takes a while to warm up. You just have to let it run and hold on until it gets warm. Other than that, great." He nodded at me. The information had been received and processed. I was so happy. I was so bad. The girls were up and organizing their things. We chatted about our planned drive down to the city of Fes and the next leg our journey. A few minutes later, I heard Mark bellow out, "Jon!" He drew it out for its full, menacing effect. A moment or two after that, he literally yelped, "Jon!" his voice raising up to a high pitched squeal. Finally, several seconds later, in his loudest voice, like a soccer radio announcer after a game winning goal, he roared out a long play "Joooonnnnnnnnn!" holding that final 'ooon' sound for several seconds. I started laughing. "What's going on?" Anna said. "What's so funny? Why is Mark yelling like that?" When I told her, both she and Sophia started to laugh. Mark walked back into the room a minute later, his normal pasty white skin had turned an alarming shade of frozen, pale albino. The look on his face was part physical pain from nearly freezing to death, and part annoyance that he had been had. There was no doubt that he hated me in that moment. He hissed at me, "I stood under that sodding shower for three sodding minutes waiting for the bloody water to get warm!" Oh my god. I fell on the floor and laughed until my stomach hurt. The girls did the same. We laughed until, literally, we just couldn't laugh anymore.

Right about then the old Moroccan women who ran the place poked her head in the doorway. She smiled at the girls and at me, and gave Mark, still scowling, a contemplative look. Then, without saying a word, she grabbed the door and dragged it away.

THE END

THE END. Really. Nothing else to see here. Seriously. Just keep moving.

You can contact Jon at jmwaldrep@gmail.com

Monkeys Wearing Pants. Copyright ©2019 Jon Waldrep

Printed in Great Britain
by Amazon